PUP AT THE PALACE

'Where's he gone?' Mandy cried desperately, looking around. Normally, she'd have loved to watch the mounted guards riding past on their sleek, beautifully groomed black horses. But now, all she could think about was the little animal. She couldn't bear to imagine him being trampled under the horses' hooves, or running out into the road and getting knocked over by a car. 'James, we have to find the puppy quickly!'

'I can't see him anywhere!' he shouted back, already separated from Mandy by a crush of people. 'He seems to have vanished!'

Frantically, they dropped their gaze and searched through the forest of legs around them for any sign of the pup. But it was hopeless – there was no trace of the little dog.

'Let's go and find Mum and Dad,' Mandy called to James. 'They can help us search. Come on, there's no time to lose!'

Animal Ark series

LUCY DANIELS

Pup
at the
Palace

Illustrations by Ann Baum

**Hodder
Children's
Books**

a division of Hodder Headline

To David Teale – a good friend to Animal Ark.

Special thanks to Jennie Walters
**Thanks also to C. J. Hall, B.Vet.Med., M.R.C.V.S., for reviewing
the veterinary information contained in this book.**

Animal Ark is a trademark of Working Partners Limited
Text copyright © 2000 Working Partners Limited
Created by Working Partners Limited, London W6 OQT
Original series created by Ben M. Baglio
Illustrations copyright © 2000 Ann Baum

First published in Great Britain in 2000
by Hodder Children's Books

For more information about Animal Ark,
please contact www.animalark.co.uk

10 9 8 7 6 5 4 3 2 1

A Catalogue record for this book is available from the British Library

ISBN 0 340 77856 3

Typeset by Avon Dataset Ltd, Bidford-on-Avon, Warks

Printed and bound in Great Britain by
Clays Ltd, St Ives plc

Hodder Children's Books
a division of Hodder Headline
338 Euston Road
London NW1 3BH

One

'Can you see anything yet, James?' Mandy Hope called eagerly across the carpark of the Fox and Goose. Pushing back her blonde hair, she shaded her eyes against the early-morning sun as she gazed over towards her friend.

'Not a sign,' James replied, turning round from his look-out post by the side of the road. 'Do you think they've forgotten about us?' he asked anxiously.

'Now don't you go alarming everyone, James Hunter!' Mandy's grandmother, Dorothy Hope, said good-naturedly. 'I phoned up to check only yesterday, and there's a coach definitely booked for eight o'clock. We've got a little while to go until then.'

'The driver won't dare to be a second late, if he knows what's good for him,' said her husband, Tom Hope, smiling at Mandy. 'You know what your grandmother's like when she's in an organising mood. Terrifying!'

As a keen member of the Welford Women's Institute, Dorothy Hope had volunteered to arrange their summer sightseeing expedition to London. It would be a wonderful way to celebrate the new century, and everyone was looking forward to seeing the Millennium Dome.

When Mandy had heard about the trip, she'd immediately thought it would be the perfect holiday for her hard-working parents – not to mention herself! Emily and Adam Hope had been rushed off their feet earlier in the summer at Animal Ark, their veterinary practice in the small Yorkshire village of Welford. Things had quietened down a little now though, so they were taking a few days off and leaving Simon, the practice nurse, in charge. They'd offered to take James to London along with them, as his parents couldn't manage to get away just then.

'Is everyone here now, Gran?' Mandy asked, looking round the group that was waiting in the carpark. She recognised lots of faces, though the people she knew best were the pet owners who came to her parents' surgery.

There was Mrs Platt, whom Mandy had helped to adopt an abandoned poodle from the animal sanctuary. She had a son in London she wanted to visit, so she'd settled the little dog, Antonia, into kennels and come along. Next to her stood Miss Davy, who lived in the Old School House and kept a flock of hens in her large garden. She looked as immaculate as ever, from the top of her silvery-grey head to the tip of her shiny brown leather shoes. Beside her, Mrs McFarlane from the post office was talking nineteen to the dozen. Her husband was staying at home, so he would be looking after their budgie, Billy, and keeping the post office and shop running smoothly.

'Let me just find my list,' said Mandy's gran, looking through a sheaf of papers in her shoulder bag. 'I think there are a few more people to come.'

'You and that list!' teased her husband affectionately. 'I should think you know it off by heart, you've looked at it so many times.'

'Well, you only have to put up with me and my list for a little while longer,' Dorothy Hope replied smartly, pulling out a dog-eared sheet of paper. 'Then you'll have total solitude for a few days.'

'Now come on, love,' Mandy's grandad replied gruffly. 'You know Smoky and I will be counting the days till you get back.'

'Are you sure you won't be too lonely without us?' Mandy asked him, suddenly picturing her grandfather and the cat all on their own in Lilac Cottage. She put her arm through his. 'If you want to come along, I'm sure it's not too late.'

Her grandfather shook his head. 'I'd better not, love,' he replied. 'The tomato plants in my greenhouse are at a very delicate stage and they'll die for certain if I leave them now. Don't you worry about me – your gran's filled the freezer with food and I'll be out in the garden from morning till night. I shall be expecting a postcard, mind.'

'I'll send you one of Buckingham Palace!' Mandy promised, before rushing over to join James. She felt too excited to stand in one place for long.

James was still looking hopefully up the road.

'Surely the coach should be coming soon!' Mandy said to him. 'I can't wait to get going, can you?'

'No,' James agreed, taking off his glasses and giving them a polish. 'Though I hope Mum and Dad remember to give Blackie lots of walks.' He'd just said goodbye to his parents and given his excitable Labrador a big farewell hug. James spent a lot of time exercising Blackie and trying to train him, and Mandy knew he would miss his dog while they were away.

'We're going to have a great time,' she said encouragingly, trying to take his mind off things. 'Just think of everything we'll be seeing – Buckingham Palace, Madame Tussaud's, Piccadilly Circus, the Tower of London—'

'And the Millennium Dome,' James reminded her as he put his glasses back on, beginning to look a bit happier. 'I really want to look at the computer displays in the Mind Zone.'

'And you should get some great photos,' Mandy said, spotting a camera at the top of James's bulging rucksack. She knew how interested he was in photography.

'I didn't want to risk bringing my best camera along, so I've only got the Polaroid,' James told her. 'Still, at least we can see the pictures straightaway. I took one of Blackie just now so I'd have something to remind me of him while we were away.' He pulled a photo out of his inside jacket pocket and showed it to Mandy.

'Oh, doesn't he look sweet!' Mandy said, smiling at Blackie's appealing face as he looked out of the picture with his head on one side. 'Come on, let's go and show Mum and Dad. We might as well sit with them till the coach comes.'

She picked up James's rucksack for him and led the way over to where her parents were sitting on one of the benches outside the pub, chatting quietly together. Her mother's long red hair glinted like a sheet of copper in the sun.

As they approached, her father broke off in an enormous yawn, raising one hand up to his beard. 'Don't worry, Dad,' Mandy said, patting his knee as she sat down next to him. 'You can have a good long sleep on the coach.' She knew her father had been up most of the night, helping a cow that had had some difficulty giving birth.

'I can't wait,' Adam Hope replied, putting his

hand over Mandy's. He looked paler than usual, and there were dark circles under his eyes. 'I could do with a holiday now, that's for sure.'

'Look at this lovely photo of Blackie that James has just taken,' Mandy said, showing her parents the picture. 'Doesn't he look cute?'

'He's got that wonderful Labrador grin on his face,' her mother said. 'They really do seem to smile sometimes, don't they?' She laughed and gave the photo back to James.

Mr and Mrs Hope loved animals just as much as Mandy did, and she often thought they must have the best job in the world. She'd learned a lot from helping them in the surgery and, one day, she hoped to be as good a vet herself. The Hopes had adopted Mandy when she was a baby, and she couldn't imagine a better home than the one she'd found with them at Animal Ark.

They had only been sitting down for a few minutes before Mandy spotted what they'd all been waiting for. A white minibus was driving slowly down the Walton road. 'At last!' she cried as it swung into the carpark. 'Now we can get moving!' She jumped to her feet and gave her father a hand up from the bench. Then she and

James grabbed their rucksacks, her father took the suitcase, and the four of them went over to join the others.

The driver opened the door and swung himself down, pushing a pair of sunglasses up on top of his head. 'Glad you're all ready and waiting,' he said, as he unlocked the luggage compartment so the cases could be loaded in. 'Traffic's building up already. I'll just pack the bags and then we'll be off. Bill's the name, by the way.' He was a small, energetic-looking man, who obviously didn't believe in wasting time chatting.

'But there are two people who haven't arrived yet,' Dorothy Hope told him, hurriedly consulting her list. 'We can't go without them.'

Bill looked at his watch. 'Well, I can't wait for ever,' he said. 'I promised to get you to London by two o'clock, so two o'clock sharp it'll be. I pride myself on my punctuality.'

'Who else is coming?' Mandy asked her grandmother.

Before she could reply, James supplied Mandy with the answer. 'Walter and Ernie!' he exclaimed in surprise.

Two elderly men were walking over from the

short row of stone cottages behind the pub, each carrying a battered, ancient-looking suitcase.

'Ah, here they are,' Dorothy Hope said with relief. 'They must have been waiting at home till they saw the coach arrive.'

'I wouldn't have thought they'd want to go to London,' Mandy whispered to James. Walter Pickard and Ernie Bell lived a few doors apart from each other and they both usually stayed close to home, apart from the occasional shopping trip into the nearby town of Walton.

'Morning, one and all,' Walter said pleasantly as they approached, touching his flat cap in greeting. He was a large, gentle man – a retired butcher who had lived on his own since his wife died. Ernie Bell just nodded briefly, eyeing the coach and its driver suspiciously. He was more difficult to get on with than Walter, though Mandy knew that his grumpy manner hid a kind heart.

'We didn't know you were interested in the big city, Mr Pickard,' James said to Walter, but it was Ernie who replied.

'Think we're past it, do you?' he growled, reluctantly letting Bill take his suitcase and wedge it on top of Miss Davy's neat zip-up bag. 'You're as bad as that Ponsonby woman. Don't *you* start going on about too much excitement being dangerous at our time of life. She's not the only one who can go gadding off down south, you know!'

Mandy tried hard not to smile. She couldn't think of anything more certain to send Ernie off to London than Mrs Ponsonby telling him he shouldn't go. Mrs Ponsonby was always bossing everyone about and giving them advice they didn't want to hear. She wasn't so good at taking advice herself, though. Mandy often told her that Pandora, her fat Pekinese, needed less food and more exercise, but it was no good. Mrs Ponsonby still gave Pandora titbits and carried her everywhere. Things had only improved a little since she'd taken in a mongrel puppy, Toby, who encouraged Pandora to run around and play like a normal dog.

Lately, Mrs Ponsonby had been more annoying than ever. She'd been invited to a garden party at Buckingham Palace because of all her work for charity. Everyone in the village had heard about it at least twenty times. Somehow, over the last few weeks, Mrs Ponsonby had managed to get the words, 'When I'm in London . . .' and 'When I meet the Queen . . .' into every conversation she had had. The garden party coincided with the WI trip but, much to everyone's relief, Mrs Ponsonby had decided to drive herself down, rather than travelling by coach with the rest of them.

'We knew there were a few spare places on the trip,' Walter explained quietly to Mandy and James, 'but we didn't really think it was our sort of thing. And then Mrs Ponsonby told Ernie that she quite understood why he didn't want to go. London was no place for an old fellow like him, set in his ways. So we decided to come after all.' He gave them a wink.

'That's great!' said Mandy, starting to climb into the minibus. 'I'm glad you did.' Then a thought suddenly occurred to her and she whirled round, nearly sending James flying. 'But who's going to look after Missie and Scraps and Tom?' Walter had three cats, and then there was Ernie's cat, Tiddles, to consider too, not to mention his pet squirrel Sammy.

'Don't you worry,' Walter reassured her. 'We wouldn't go off and abandon them. That young lad from the pub is calling in twice a day to feed them, and he's in charge of Tiddles and Sammy, too. He came round yesterday and we showed him where everything was.'

'Of course! John's back now, isn't he?' Mandy remembered.

John Hardy was the son of Julian Hardy, the landlord of the Fox and Goose, and he came back to Welford from boarding-school every holiday. Living so close by, he was the ideal person to look after Walter and Ernie's pets.

'John's certainly going to be busy,' Miss Davy said briskly. 'He's feeding my hens as well, and shutting them up for the night. I hope he's going to take his duties seriously.'

Bang on cue, an upstairs window in the pub flew open, and John Hardy's tousled head emerged. As he waved to them, Mandy felt a twinge of jealousy. She'd have loved being in charge of all those animals! A fresh surge of excitement soon stopped her feeling too envious, though.

When everyone was finally on board, Bill checked his watch again and they set off. The minibus pulled slowly out of the carpark and started down the road on its long journey to London.

They had only driven a short distance when Bill suddenly gave a shout of alarm and slammed on the brakes so sharply that all the passengers were thrown forward. The book Miss Davy had just opened flew across the aisle, James lost his headphones and Mrs McFarlane nearly choked on her peppermint.

James leaned round the seats in front to look through the windscreen, then nudged Mandy without speaking. He pointed up ahead, and she followed his glance. In the middle of the road stood none other than Mrs Ponsonby herself, puffing and panting and red in the face. She had a large suitcase and a hatbox at her feet. Her Peke, Pandora, was tucked under one arm, and she was waving the minibus down with the other.

'Stop this bus!' she shouted loudly.

Two

'Really, driver!' Mrs Ponsonby said severely after Bill had opened the minibus door. 'What kind of speed is that for a narrow country lane? You nearly ran me down! Now, please take my luggage, but do be careful. The hat in this box is an original design.'

Bill gave her a long look, as though deciding whether to reply, and then shook his head. Glancing at his watch, he grumbled, 'No time to open the boot. You'll have to keep your case with you.' He yanked up the suitcase and stowed it between the seats. Mrs Ponsonby clicked her tongue in annoyance, then picked up her hatbox, clutched Pandora more firmly, and prepared to climb on board.

'Gran! You didn't tell us Mrs Ponsonby was coming,' Mandy hissed through to the seats in front, where her grandmother was sitting on her own.

'I didn't know she was!' came Dorothy Hope's horrified reply.

'Here – you can't bring that animal on to my minibus!' Bill told Mrs Ponsonby, having just noticed Pandora. 'What if it messes on the floor?'

'Pandora is not just an "animal", she is a pedigree Pekinese,' Mrs Ponsonby announced grandly. 'And she does not "mess" on the floor, I can assure you.' She pushed past him indignantly and sank into the empty seat next to Dorothy Hope.

Bill shook his head again. 'You'd better be right,' he muttered doubtfully, starting the engine and preparing to drive off.

'Poor Gran!' Mandy whispered to James, pulling a sympathetic face. She knew Mrs Ponsonby really got on her grandmother's nerves. Now she would have to sit beside her all the way to London, with no chance of escape.

'I thought Mrs Ponsonby was driving down later,' James whispered back. 'What's she doing here now?'

Together, they listened as Mrs Ponsonby explained to Dorothy Hope. 'I'd decided to take the doggies out for a little drive last night, but – would you believe it – the car just wouldn't start! And who knows if I could have got it fixed in time to drive to London on Monday. One simply can't take any risks when one is meeting the Queen!' She laughed and patted her hat, while Mrs Hope murmured something Mandy couldn't hear.

'Anyway,' Mrs Ponsonby went on, 'I remembered there were some spare places on your little expedition. By that time, it was too late to phone you and check, and I must have just missed you when I rang this morning. So Pandora and I set off to meet you on the road! How lucky there's an empty seat next to you, Dorothy. We can chat all the way.'

'Very lucky,' Mandy's gran echoed faintly.

'But where's Toby, Mrs Ponsonby?' Mandy asked, undoing her safety belt for a few seconds and leaning over the top of the seats to give Pandora a quick pat.

'Oh, I've left him with my sister,' she replied, turning round to smile graciously at Mandy. 'Toby is a delightful creature, of course, but he might be a little – shall we say – unpredictable, staying in a hotel. Not to mention at Buckingham Palace! I'm afraid the excitement would be too much for him. He might forget himself.'

Mandy caught James's eye and they both collapsed into giggles behind the seat backs at the thought of Toby forgetting himself during a garden party at Buckingham Palace.

'What about your hotel?' Mandy's gran asked Mrs Ponsonby, as though an alarming thought had just occurred to her. 'Can they fit you in over the weekend? I'm afraid our bed and breakfast is fully booked – Walter and Ernie are having to stay in a pub round the corner.'

'Don't worry about that, my dear,' came the reply. 'I phoned the hotel last night and they can squeeze us in for a few extra nights. After all, I don't really think a bed and breakfast is quite our sort of place, is it, Pandora? And as for a pub . . .' She shuddered.

'Well, I think it's great here,' Mandy said,

bouncing on the bed in the twin room she was sharing with her grandmother. 'Good choice, Gran!'

The Welford party were staying in small hotels, pubs or guest houses in Greenwich, not far from the Millennium Dome. Dorothy Hope had booked her family and friends into a large Victorian house called The Crow's-Nest in one of the narrow streets near the river. Mandy had held her breath as Bill steered the minibus expertly through the traffic. There were so many cars, and so many people! It was all very different from the quiet green fields and country lanes of Welford.

'There you are,' Bill said, as he parked opposite the guest house and checked his watch again. 'Five to two. By the time I've unloaded all your luggage, it'll be two o'clock precisely!'

Inside The Crow's-Nest, everything was ordered and calm. The place was run by a fair-haired Scotsman with a bristly ginger beard, who introduced himself as 'Alexander McPherson, though everyone calls me Mac'. He showed them all to their rooms before starting to take their luggage upstairs. Mandy's parents had a double room with a four-poster bed, which they were delighted with. Eileen Davy and Mrs McFarlane were sharing a twin room, while James was on his own next door to Mandy and her grandmother. Mrs Platt was staying with her son over in Wimbledon, though she was going to meet up with the others for their trip to the Millennium Dome.

'If you don't mind, love,' Dorothy said, sitting on the other bed, 'I think I'll have a bit of a rest now. Six hours of Mrs Ponsonby has nearly finished me off. Why don't you and James go exploring?'

'OK, Gran,' Mandy said. 'I can understand just how you feel!'

She shut the door quietly behind her and set off down the corridor to find James. Just like the bedrooms, its walls were hung with old maps and prints of sailing ships.

James's room was full of model boats, too. 'I bet Mac's been a sailor at one time or another,' Mandy commented, picking up an ornament on the chest of drawers. It was a bottle, with a tiny ship sailing along inside it. 'How on earth did that get in there?' she wondered, fascinated.

James shrugged. 'Well, he certainly loves the

sea,' he said, laying his books out on the bedside table. 'Did you see the ship's wheel at the top of the stairs?'

Mandy nodded. 'Shall we go and explore when you've finished unpacking?' she said, putting down the bottle. After hours of sitting still on the coach, she felt like stretching her legs.

A few minutes later, they walked along the landing, past the huge oak wheel and down the staircase. James paused to look at a large print hanging at the bottom of the stairs. 'So that's what Greenwich was like three hundred years ago,' he said to Mandy, reading the caption beneath the picture. 'Look at all those ships on the Thames!'

'Aye, the river was a busy old place,' said Mac, who was just about to take the last of the suitcases upstairs. 'There's been many a king and queen of England who'd sail up river to Greenwich, and bring the whole court with them too. Henry VIII was born here, you know, and Elizabeth I used to spend the summers at Greenwich.'

Mandy glanced round the crowded hall. There were so many things to look at! Wooden seagulls, which were suspended from the ceiling, flapped their wings gracefully when she and James pulled their cords. In one corner stood a big iron-bound chest and above it were shelves crammed with what looked like old navigational instruments – a brass telescope, a compass and others Mandy couldn't identify. Shells and crystals were on display, too, and a huge shark's jawbone. Mac put down the luggage he was carrying and came over to the two friends when he noticed them looking at it.

'Did you know a shark's teeth were arranged in rows?' he said, taking the jawbone off the shelf to show it to them. 'So if the creature loses one, another grows forward from behind to take its place.'

Mandy shivered, examining the sharp, jagged teeth. 'They're vicious!' she said.

'Too right,' Mac smiled, picking up the bags and setting off upstairs again. 'Once a shark's got hold of you, you won't get away in a hurry.'

Mandy was examining a bundle of wooden walking-sticks carved with animal heads, when all of a sudden she heard a squeaky little miaow. 'Did you hear that?' she asked James, staring eagerly all around. 'I think there's a cat here somewhere!' A real animal, rather than a carved or painted one, would make The Crow's-Nest just perfect as far as she was concerned.

'There it is!' James said quietly, nudging Mandy and pointing towards a large globe in another corner. Peeping shyly out from behind it was a small tortoiseshell cat. Its tawny fur was striped with ginger, brown and black, and its large golden eyes were as round as saucers.

'I thought so!' Mandy said, dropping to her knees and smiling at the cat. She held out her hand and called in a soft, encouraging voice, 'Come on, then, puss! Come and say hello.'

The tortoiseshell gave another reedy miaow and ventured out from behind the globe. Mandy scrabbled on the rug with her fingers and the cat bounded over, pouncing on her hand and batting it with soft paws.

'Oh, isn't she lovely!' Mandy said, grinning up at James as she played with the little creature.

'How do you know it's a she?' James asked, crouching down beside Mandy.

'Tortoiseshells are nearly always female,' Mandy said, hoping she didn't sound too much of a know-all. 'We had a male tortoiseshell in the surgery the other day with fur balls, but Dad told me they are really rare.' She scratched the cat below her ears and she began to purr, pushing her head into Mandy's hand as she stroked the soft, thick fur. Then, with a wave of her tail, she wandered away across the hall to a half-open door. Looking back at them, she miaowed again.

'Looks like she wants us to follow her,' Mandy said, getting to her feet. 'Perhaps we're going to get a guided tour!'

She went after the cat into what looked like a dining-room, full of tables and chairs. The little tortoiseshell dived under one of the tables and began to play with the trailing edge of the tablecloth, rolling on to her back again and clutching the fabric fiercely with sharp claws.

'Careful!' Mandy said, disentangling the cloth. 'You'll tear it and then Mac won't be pleased.'

'Look at that, Mandy!' James said behind her, and she followed his pointing finger. Mounted on the opposite wall was a huge, painted wooden bust of a woman. She was staring into the distance with large unseeing eyes, and long dark hair streaming out behind her as though blown by some invisible wind. The name 'Daisy May' was painted in flowing golden script on the blue shawl draped round her neck.

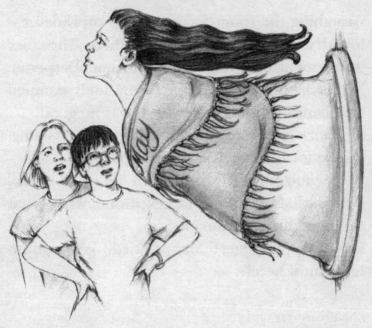

'Wow! That must be an old ship's figurehead,' Mandy said, awestruck. 'It looks like she's bursting through the wall and heading straight for us. Spooky, isn't it?'

But before James could reply, there was a sudden explosion of noise. A loud, harsh voice came ringing through the air. 'Goodbye!' it shouted menacingly. 'Time to go!'

'What's that?' James cried, grabbing Mandy's arm. 'Who's there?'

'I don't know,' she replied desperately,

searching the room for some sign of whoever –
or whatever – was screaming at them. The voice
rang out again, even louder this time. Desperate
to block out the terrifying noise, Mandy clamped
her hands over her ears. But it was no good.

'Everybody's gone home!' it shrieked this time.
'Time for bed! Night-night, sleep tight!'

The tortoiseshell cat streaked out of the room,
leaving Mandy and James alone with what
sounded like a madman.

'Come on, James!' Mandy cried. 'We've got to
get out of here!'

Three

'Look behind you!' screamed the invisible voice. Mandy and James whirled round, but there was nobody there.

'Who's that?' Mandy called as bravely as she could, beginning to feel angry now, as well as frightened. Somebody seemed to be having a joke at their expense, and it wasn't very funny.

'Daisy May is a wicked woman,' the voice said in a lower, plaintive tone.

'Wh-where are you?' James cried uncertainly. 'Come out and show yourself!'

'Have a nice day,' the voice mocked, and then

cackled. Mandy and James heard another peal of laughter behind them. They turned round to see a tall girl of about their age, with shoulder-length brown hair, watching them from the doorway with an amused look on her face.

'What's going on?' Mandy demanded, feeling slightly stupid and loosening James's grip on her arm.

'Looks like you've just met Sinbad for the first time,' the girl replied. She walked into the room and pointed towards one dark corner. There, in the shadows, stood a big cage on wheels. Inside it, a grey bird was walking delicately along the thick tree branch that served as a perch.

'So he was the one making all that noise?' Mandy said, scarcely able to believe her eyes. Her heart was still thumping madly and her palms prickled with sweat. 'Do you mean we've just been frightened half to death by a *parrot*?'

She and James went up to the birdcage for a closer look. Sinbad was slate grey, apart from his scarlet tail and the silvery white mask around his small yellow eyes. The feathers on his neck were edged in a paler shade, so that each one looked distinct and separate. Mandy thought he was just as beautiful as some of the more brightly-coloured birds she'd seen.

'Hello, Sinbad,' she said cautiously, but the parrot seemed to have decided he'd done enough talking. He stared silently at her and then sank his head down between his shoulders, ruffling up the feathers.

'He's not very friendly, is he?' James said to the girl, who'd come up to the cage beside them. 'Doesn't he like meeting strangers?'

'I asked Mac about him yesterday, when we arrived,' she replied. 'He said Sinbad's feeling very grumpy at the moment, for some reason, and it's best not to take too much notice. My name's Casey Baxter, by the way. I'm on holiday over here, from New York.'

James and Mandy introduced themselves too, and then Mandy turned back to the parrot in his cage. She couldn't help wondering why Sinbad was so hostile. 'He's a great talker,' she said to Casey. 'I wonder if we can teach him anything more friendly to say.'

'Something tells me he's not in a very friendly mood,' Casey replied.

They watched as Sinbad made his way over to

the container of seeds at the side of his cage and picked up a monkey nut with his foot. He cracked the shell with his strong curved beak and used his tongue to help take out the nut inside. James whistled the parrot a tune, but Sinbad only glared at him suspiciously.

'Let's leave him to sulk for the moment,' Casey said to them. 'Have you seen the garden yet? Come on, I'll show you.'

They said goodbye to Sinbad and left him in the quiet dining-room. 'We'll come and see you again soon,' Mandy promised, thinking the parrot looked rather forlorn as they left. She made up her mind to ask Mac all about him.

'This is such a cool place,' Casey told them as they went along a corridor to the back door. 'My dad's a doctor, and someone who works at the hospital with him visited London last year. He told us we just had to stay here.'

'Do you know why the house is so full of boats and sailing things?' Mandy asked.

'Oh, that's because Mac used to be a ship's cook,' Casey replied, opening the door on to a small courtyard garden at the back of the house. 'Just wait till you see breakfast tomorrow!' she added, walking down a cobbled path to a blue-painted bench. 'You won't need to eat again for the rest of the day, I'm telling you.'

'Have you had a look around Greenwich yet?' asked James, sitting down beside her.

'Yes, I have,' Casey said. 'We got up early this morning. There's so much to see! The park, and the Observatory, and a couple of palaces, and this wonderful ship called the Cutty Sark. It's amazing – full of figureheads like old Daisy May in the dining-room. Hey, maybe I could show it to you this afternoon? And then tomorrow we're going to see them Changing the Guard at Buckingham Palace. You'll have to come with us – if you'd like to, that is. We're going to Madame Tussaud's in the afternoon, but you have to book tickets otherwise you'll be lining up for a year, Mom says.'

'Slow down,' Mandy laughed. 'You're making me feel tired!' She gazed around the garden. To her delight, there was the tortoiseshell cat, lying in a sunny spot beneath a rosemary bush. She walked over to say hello. The cat got to her feet, arched her back, and then twined around Mandy's legs, miaowing.

'That's Patch,' Casey called over. 'She's beautiful, isn't she?'

'Lovely!' Mandy replied, picking Patch up and burying her face in the cat's soft, warm fur. She suddenly felt quite certain that they couldn't have found a nicer place to stay in the whole of London.

The next day, it was time to start sightseeing. The Hopes met Casey's parents over a huge cooked breakfast that morning, and they were soon getting on so well they decided to spend the day together.

'That's awesome!' Casey said to Mandy a few hours later as they gazed between tall iron railings at the imposing sight of Buckingham Palace stretched out in front of them. 'So this is where the Queen lives when she's in London, right? Do you think she's looking down on us at this very moment?'

'She might be,' James said. He pointed up to a red and gold flag fluttering against the blue sky. 'Look, the Royal Standard's flying. When she's not at the Palace, they put up the Union Jack instead. I was reading all about it in my guidebook last night.'

'Wow!' Casey grinned. She waved her arm towards the empty balcony. 'How d'you do, Your Majesty? This is Casey Baxter from New York, just dropping by to say hello!'

Mandy turned to watch all the people around them. Tour guides held up different coloured umbrellas so they could be seen by their groups, families posed for photographs and hot-dog sellers jostled for the best position. Mandy wrinkled her nose. The frying onions smelled delicious but, as a vegetarian, she wasn't tempted by the sausages.

All of a sudden, she spotted something she hadn't expected to see. Sitting near one of the hot-dog stands was an adorable, chocolate-brown Labrador puppy, head cocked to one side as it stared longingly up at the sausages. Mandy looked at the pup more closely, and then gazed at the people standing around it. No one seemed to be taking much notice of the little dog, but she felt sure its owner was somewhere nearby. An animal as young as that wouldn't have been left to wander around alone in the middle of London.

Casey was still engrossed in what was happening at the Palace, so Mandy nudged James.

'Look!' she said. 'There's a puppy over there, and it seems to be all on its own. Do you think it's run away from someone?'

'Oh, isn't it lovely?' James said as he spotted the cute little pup. 'You're right, though – there doesn't seem to be anybody looking after it. Is it wearing a collar?'

'I'm not sure,' Mandy said, narrowing her eyes as she stared over. 'We're too far away to tell. Come on, let's go a bit nearer and find out what's happening.'

'Where are you going? You'll lose your place!' Casey called after them from her look-out post by the railings, but James and Mandy were already hurrying off.

'We'll be back in a second,' Mandy called over her shoulder. There was no time to explain.

'I think I've got something that might help us catch the puppy if we need to,' James said, searching his jacket pockets as they threaded their way through the crowd. 'Yes! Here it is!' Triumphantly, he pulled out an ancient-looking dog biscuit. 'Left over from one of Blackie's obedience classes,' he explained.

'Great!' Mandy said, her eyes fixed on the

puppy. Some people in the crowd were glancing at it from time to time and smiling, but most of them were too busy waiting for something to happen at the Palace to pay the pup much attention.

'It's not trailing a lead,' James said as they approached. 'I don't even think it's wearing a collar.'

'And it's definitely alone,' Mandy added. 'We'd better try and catch it, in case it takes off into the traffic.' She crouched down a little way off, not wanting to frighten the young animal away, and clapped her hands on her thighs to attract its attention. 'Come on,' she called cheerfully. 'There's a good dog! Look what we've got for you!'

The pup looked up at the sound of her voice and raised its soft brown ears inquiringly. 'That's the way!' James called encouragingly, holding out the dog biscuit. 'Over here!'

The puppy gave a short bark and bounded towards them, ears pricked and tail wagging furiously at the sight – and smell – of food. 'You're hungry, aren't you?' Mandy said, as she watched it wolf down the biscuit James was offering.

'Labrador puppies are always hungry,' James

said smiling, as the pup licked his hand with a rough pink tongue. 'Do you remember what Blackie was like when he was small? He'd eat anything in sight! And this puppy looks like it's smiling at us, just like Blackie does. Do you think it's male or female?'

'Hard to tell for sure,' Mandy replied, as she watched the puppy frisking around. 'It won't keep still for long enough, but I think it's a male dog, don't you? Mum and Dad can tell us if I'm right.'

The young dog had lost his fat baby tummy, but he still had that soft, puppyish look around the face and seemed not quite able to control his long legs yet. Mandy patted his silky brown fur and the pup pushed a damp, cold nose into her hand.

'He doesn't look like a stray,' James said. 'His coat's in fantastic condition.'

Mandy stroked one of the puppy's soft ears and he gazed adoringly up at her with melting brown eyes. 'No, I think you've got a good home somewhere, haven't you?' she asked. 'And we've got to get you back there!'

The puppy gave another short bark and began to dash around them, wagging his tail furiously and crouching down on his front legs, waiting for

James and Mandy to join in the game.

'Quick, James!' Mandy cried, unbuckling the belt around her jeans so she could use it as a temporary lead. 'We have to catch him before he runs off again!'

'Let me just get a photo,' James said, already looking through the viewfinder of his camera. The puppy stared inquisitively back at him.

And then disaster struck. A mounted policewoman on a dapple-grey horse rode up to the hot-dog sellers. 'Clear this area immediately!' she said in a loud voice. 'You've been told a hundred times not to operate here. It's illegal. Go on, off you go – right now. There are horses coming and you'd better not get in the way!'

At once, everyone in the crowd surged forward, cameras at the ready, to get a good look at the Household Cavalry who were riding down past Buckingham Palace on the way back to their barracks in Hyde Park. Grumbling, the hot-dog sellers began to wheel their trolleys away through the throng. But in all the chaos, the puppy disappeared.

'Where's he gone?' Mandy cried desperately, looking around. Normally, she'd have loved to watch the mounted guards riding past on their sleek, beautifully groomed black horses. But now, all she could think about was the little animal. She couldn't bear to imagine him being trampled under the horses' hooves, or running out into the road and getting knocked over by a car. 'James, we have to find the puppy quickly!'

'I can't see him anywhere!' he shouted back, already separated from Mandy by a crush of people. 'He seems to have vanished!'

Frantically, they dropped their gaze and searched through the forest of legs around them

for any sign of the pup. But it was hopeless – there was no trace of the little dog.

'Let's go and find Mum and Dad,' Mandy called to James. 'They can help us search. Come on, there's no time to lose!'

'I don't think there's anything more we can do for now,' Emily Hope said, putting a comforting arm round Mandy's shoulders. 'I don't want you and James getting lost in the crowd as well – that won't help anybody. Let's wait until it starts to thin out, and then we'll be able to spot this puppy of yours. Why don't you go and watch with Casey for the moment?'

'OK,' Mandy said disconsolately. 'I suppose it might take our mind off things. We'll see you back here when Changing the Guard is finished.'

It took James and Mandy a while to make their way through the packed crowd of tourists. Eventually, though, they spotted Casey's baseball cap and managed to join her by the railings at the front, where the best views were to be had.

'What happened to you two?' she asked.

'We spotted this little lost puppy by a hot-dog stand,' Mandy explained miserably, 'but he ran away before we could catch him.'

'Oh, no!' Casey said, giving Mandy a sympathetic pat on the back. 'When the display is over, I'll help you search some more. Look, here come the new guards!'

A group of soldiers in scarlet and black uniforms had appeared on the Palace forecourt and were marching towards the sentry boxes. Mandy was more interested in looking at the wide pavement behind her, though, just in case she spotted a flash of brown fur or a waving tail.

Suddenly Casey grabbed her arm. 'That puppy!' she asked excitedly. 'It wasn't a chocolate brown Lab, by any chance, was it?'

'Yes, it was!' Mandy replied eagerly. 'Why? Have you seen him?'

'Looks like he's just joined up for guard duty,' Casey grinned. 'Here, pull yourself up next to me, so you can watch.'

Mandy hoisted herself up by the railings and peered through. 'I don't believe it!' she exclaimed. A few paces behind the guards was their missing puppy, walking along proudly, his tail held high.

'He must have slipped through the railings,' James said, climbing up beside the two girls.

All around them, people had begun laughing and pointing at the puppy, talking excitedly in what sounded like twenty different languages. The guards didn't seem to have noticed they had a new recruit, and the pup was careful to keep a few paces behind them. When they reached the first sentry box, the little dog quickly nipped behind it. For a few seconds there was nothing to be seen, but then a mischievous brown head peeped round the corner. The soldiers were so intent on changing over guard duty that none of them spotted it. Everyone else had, though, and a loud gale of laughter rose up in the air.

'Naughty little thing!' Mandy smiled. 'He obviously thinks it's a wonderful game.'

Excited by the noise, the puppy decided he had had enough of marching and began to twirl around, chasing his tail. Then he bounded off through an archway that led to a courtyard within the Palace and disappeared from sight. There was a loud round of applause from the crowd.

'Well!' said James, chuckling. 'At least now we know he's safely away from the road.'

'I suppose so,' Mandy said doubtfully. 'I just hope he'll be OK in there.' She stared up at the long rows of windows, imagining the vast number of rooms inside the Palace, and frowned. The little dog might have found his way in, but would he ever manage to find a way out again?

Four

The next morning, Mandy was the first person down to the dining-room. Mac was apparently in the middle of laying the breakfast tables, but he had stopped for a moment by the birdcage.

'Morning!' Mandy said, going over to join him. 'How's Sinbad today?'

'He's calmed down a bit since yesterday,' said Mac, turning away and starting to put out the cereal bowls. 'I'm sorry he gave you such a fright. Casey told me all about it last night.'

'That's OK,' Mandy replied, watching Sinbad flex his long toes and walk delicately along the wooden perch. 'I think his voice is wonderful. I've never heard anything like it!'

'I wish all my guests agreed with you,' Mac told her with a smile. 'Sinbad's an amazing mimic, like lots of African Greys, but some people don't find him very funny.'

'Oh no, I bet they don't,' Mandy said. She could just imagine what Mrs Ponsonby would say if Sinbad imitated her! The parrot cocked his head coyly and looked sideways at her out of one yellow eye. 'He does seem happier today,' she went on, watching as Sinbad began to preen his soft grey feathers carefully. 'Do you think he'd let me take him out of the cage?'

'A couple of months ago, I'd have said yes straightaway.' Mac sighed, folding a napkin. 'But now I think it would be better not to risk it. He might take a swipe at you, and that beak is very sharp!' He finished with the pile of linen and then took some grapes from a bowl on the sideboard. 'Here, why don't I take him out and you can give him some fruit?' he suggested. 'If you'd like to, that is. You seem very interested in him.'

'Oh, I am!' Mandy replied. 'My parents are vets

and that's what I'd like to be too, if I can get the right grades. I've never met an African Grey before.'

'They're very intelligent birds,' Mac said, passing her the grapes and opening the cage door. 'They can be nervous, but I've had Sinbad since he was a chick and tamed him myself.' He stretched his hand into the cage and Sinbad hopped on to his finger, chirping and whistling excitedly.

'I think he's beautiful,' Mandy said, enjoying a good look at Sinbad out in the open. He watched Mac, turning his head this way and that, and seemed to listen intently as his owner talked to him. 'He has so many different expressions, doesn't he?' Mandy went on, offering the parrot a grape. 'Like he's thinking all the time.'

'You're right,' Mac agreed. 'And you should see him when he's about to sing! He ruffles up his neck feathers and looks very grand, like he's some famous Italian tenor!' They both laughed, and watched as Sinbad carefully took the grape with one claw and raised it to his beak to nibble. 'He doesn't sing much these days, though,' Mac added quietly.

'Do you know why he's so miserable at the moment?' Mandy asked. She couldn't hear about an unhappy animal without wanting to help.

Mac shook his head. 'I don't know what's got into him,' he said anxiously. 'I've taken him to the vet for a check-up, but there isn't anything physically wrong. He just doesn't seem himself at all – he's so moody! He won't talk half as much as he used to, and when he does, he can be very aggressive – like he was with you yesterday. But the worst thing is, he's started pulling out his feathers. Look, just there.'

'Oh, yes, so he has!' Mandy said. Several of the overlapping dark grey feathers on Sinbad's breast were missing, revealing the fluffy white down beneath. 'Why would he do that?' she asked.

Mac frowned. 'I've got no idea,' he answered, putting Sinbad carefully back into the cage and shutting the door. 'I make sure he doesn't have mites and I spray him with water so his skin doesn't get too dry. I wish he'd stop, though. The vet told me it's a habit that can quickly get out of control – some birds pluck their skin bare.'

'Oh, how horrible!' Mandy exclaimed. It was awful to think of Sinbad deliberately hurting himself. He obviously had lots of love and attention, so why should he need to do such a thing? 'I'll ask Mum and Dad if there's anything we can do,' she told Mac. 'I'm sure they'll come up with something.'

Mandy didn't get a chance to talk to her mother about Sinbad until later that morning, when they were sitting on a boat together, sailing down the Thames. Mandy's gran had suggested at breakfast that a trip down the river from Greenwich to Westminster would be a good way of seeing the sights. It was a lovely sunny morning, and everyone thought going out on the water was a wonderful idea. Walter and Ernie had met up with them at Greenwich Pier, which was just around the corner from the pub where they were staying, and Casey and her parents had come along too. Dr and Mrs Baxter were getting on so well with the Hopes that it seemed natural for them all to go sightseeing together again.

Mrs Hope was not too encouraging about Sinbad's prospects. 'Feather plucking can turn into a serious problem very quickly,' she said gravely. 'There could be any number of explanations. Sinbad's skin might be irritated, or he might be under some kind of stress, or bored, or even ready for a mate. I'm happy to have a look at him, but often there's no physical reason for that kind of behaviour. You have to get to know the bird to find out why he's doing it.'

'Well then, maybe that's what we should do,' James said. Mandy had told him all about Sinbad's problem, and he'd been listening in on the conversation with her mum. 'Between us, we should be able to help him before we have to go back home.'

'I don't know,' Mrs Hope said, smiling at them both. 'First puppies, now parrots! I thought we'd left all our patients back in Welford! Just don't let worrying about Sinbad spoil your holiday.'

'We'll try not to,' Mandy promised. If there was an animal somewhere in need of help, though, she and James wouldn't rest until they'd found a solution. And Mandy's mum was just the same, no matter what she might say.

'Look – straight ahead!' James said suddenly,

focusing his binoculars on the river. 'That was a cormorant, wasn't it?'

'You're right,' Mr Hope said from his seat a little further up the boat. 'There's another one sitting on that post over there. See how it holds its wings outstretched to dry them?'

'Here, have a look through these for a minute,' James said to Mandy, passing her the binoculars.

'Thanks, James,' Mandy replied, peering through them at the dark bird zigzagging down the river in front of them. Suddenly it dipped down to the water and flew back up with a flash of silver in its beak. 'Oh, it's caught something!' she exclaimed, before handing the binoculars on to Casey so she could see too.

'There's all kinds of fish coming back to the Thames now the water's so much cleaner,' the riverboat captain told them, leaning out of his cabin. 'You can even catch a salmon if you're lucky.'

The recorded commentary crackled into life to tell everyone the boat was approaching Tower Bridge, and that the Tower of London would soon be in full view on their right. They should look out for Traitors' Gate, where condemned prisoners were brought into the Tower by boat from the courts at Westminster. This would have been the last glimpse of the outside world, for most of them.

'I can't wait to look round the Tower,' Casey said, as they sailed past the grim, forbidding building. 'That's where the Crown Jewels are, right? And the execution block where they beheaded one of Henry VIII's wives?'

Mandy shivered – it all sounded very gloomy to her. As far as she was concerned, it was much more fun to be out in the sunshine on the river.

'That's right. We're going right down as far as Westminster Pier now, but we can stop off on the way back,' Mr Hope promised. 'After we've taken a look at Big Ben and Westminster Abbey. And maybe had a quick pizza,' he added hopefully.

'Dad!' Mandy said, outraged. 'On top of that huge breakfast? You'll have to go back on a diet when this holiday's over!'

'I've never eaten a pizza in my life, and I don't intend to start now,' Ernie declared. 'A sandwich in the park will suit Walter and me, thank you very much. There was a brass band playing there yesterday lunch-time. Not as good as some I've heard up North, mind you.'

'But think what Mrs Ponsonby would say, if she heard you'd had pizza for lunch!' James said innocently. 'She couldn't call you set in your ways then, could she, Mr Bell?' He caught Mandy's eye and she had to bite her lip hard to stop herself from smiling.

Ernie thought for a while. 'Maybe not,' he said eventually. 'I shall have to see how I feel.'

'Speaking of Mrs Ponsonby,' Mandy's gran broke in, 'she rang up The Crow's-Nest last night. I think she's rather lonely in that smart hotel of hers. Anyway, she's invited us all to lunch tomorrow.'

'But we're going to look round the Royal Mews tomorrow!' Mandy protested. 'Dad promised he'd take us.' On their way back from Buckingham Palace the day before, James had spotted a sign for the Royal Mews, 'the largest working stable in London'. It was closed at the weekend, but Mandy, James and Casey all wanted to go back there on Monday. A chance to see the Queen's magnificent carriage horses close up was just too good to miss. And besides, they might be able to ask someone if a Labrador puppy had been found anywhere in the Palace. Mandy was counting on that!

'Don't worry,' her grandmother reassured her. 'I suggested we should all meet up for a picnic in St James's Park. It's just opposite the Palace, so you won't have to miss out on anything.'

'And we can take Pandora for a walk,' James said. 'I bet Mrs Ponsonby hasn't been exercising her properly.'

'Oh, James, that's a great idea,' Mandy said, beaming at him. 'Who knows, we might even get Dad to go jogging!'

'Mum, Dad, after we've seen Westminster Abbey, do you think we could go to the viewing tower in Westminster Cathedral?' Mandy asked, looking up from James's guide book. They were all standing beside Big Ben, waiting for James to finish trying to photograph the clock face. 'It's in Victoria Street, where the shops are,' she went on, 'so I'm sure there'll be a restaurant near by.'

'Well, OK, as long as the Baxters are happy with that,' Mr Hope replied. 'I didn't realise you were so keen on sightseeing, love.'

On their way over to the cathedral, Mandy

explained her plan to James and Casey. 'According to James's book, you can see right into the gardens at Buckingham Palace from the top of the tower,' she said as they walked along the empty Sunday-morning street. 'I know it's a long shot, but if we can get a good view . . .'

'. . . We might be able to spot that Labrador puppy we saw yesterday,' James finished off for her, slinging the binoculars round his neck.

'Exactly!' Mandy said. She knew that James wouldn't have forgotten the little dog either. The puppy had probably been found by now, but there was a slim chance it might still be running round the Palace grounds. Perhaps if they spotted it, they could alert one of the police officers by the gate. At the very least, it would be good to see the pup again and make sure it was safe.

They soon reached the cathedral, set back from the road with a large paved area in front. Mrs Hope put her finger to her lips as they went through the huge doors, because there was a church service going on. They made their way quietly to the lift that would take them up to the viewing platform.

'Well, that's a real English lift,' Dr Baxter said

as its doors opened. 'It's half the size of our elevators! We won't all fit in.'

'Why don't I take the young 'uns up first?' the attendant suggested. 'It's quite safe at the top – you can't fall out.'

'Good idea!' Mandy said at once. She knew her mother felt she should stop worrying about animals and just enjoy the holiday, so it would be much better if they had a few minutes on their own to look for the pup.

The view from the top of the tower might have been spectacular, but it was a big disappointment as far as they were concerned. 'Maybe you could see into the Palace gardens ten years ago,' James said, squinting through his binoculars, 'but you certainly can't now. There's a great big office block in the way!'

Mandy sighed as she looked towards Buckingham Palace. She could just see the golden top of the Victoria monument outside its gates and the green trees in St James's Park, but that was about it. There was no way they could look into the gardens, even with binoculars. And then, suddenly, a flurry of activity beneath them caught her eye. Some tourists were milling about in the square below, while a small shape ran to and fro around their group. A small brown shape . . .

'James! Casey! Look down there, where those people are,' she cried excitedly. 'I think it might be the puppy!'

'Where?' Casey demanded, squeezing in beside her and peering down. 'I can't see where you mean. Hang on a minute . . . ! Yes! You're right – that's him!'

'Looks like he's playing with somebody,' James added over her shoulder. 'Or maybe chasing a pigeon.'

'Well then, what are we waiting for? Come on, let's see if we can get him!' Mandy cried, already rushing out. 'Quick, before he runs off again!'

Casey's parents and the Hopes were just getting out of the lift as Mandy, James and Casey arrived to take it back down. 'We've had a good look,' Mandy told her parents quickly as the three of them squeezed into the lift. 'See you downstairs, outside the cathedral.'

'What's going on?' Mrs Baxter asked. 'Why are you in such a hurry?'

'We'll explain later,' Casey promised as the lift doors closed and the surprised attendant started taking them back to ground level.

'Come on, lift,' Mandy groaned as they creaked slowly downwards. 'Hurry up! I couldn't bear it if we lost the puppy again. We're so close now!'

Eventually the doors opened. They walked through the quiet cathedral as quickly as they could without running, and then out into the square. 'Oh no!' James cried in dismay. 'Where's he gone?' The group of tourists were scattering towards the street, and there was no sign of the little dog anywhere among them.

'We're looking for the puppy that was here just now,' Mandy said to a large man in sunglasses at the back of the group. 'Did you see where he went?' But he just smiled and waved at her, obviously not understanding a word.

'There he is!' Casey shouted suddenly. 'Look, down that little back road!' She rushed across the square and then stepped out to cross the side road – straight into the path of a black London taxi. There was a horrible squeal of brakes, followed by the even more terrifying noise of a heavy thud as Casey's body hit the front of the cab.

'Casey!' Mandy screamed, running towards

her. 'James, go back and get Dr Baxter – and hurry!'

Five

Mandy flew across the pavement towards Casey, her heart pounding and her eyes fixed on the slumped body. Casey had been thrown back by the force of the collision, and was now lying, terrifyingly still, on the pavement. As Mandy approached, though, she saw Casey begin to struggle up on one elbow.

'No! Stop!' she cried, kneeling beside her. 'Just stay here – don't try to get up.' She knew from experience with animals who'd been run over that a patient shouldn't be moved before getting medical attention. That could do further damage to broken bones or back injuries.

The taxi driver came rushing over to join them, his face as pale as Casey's. 'Is she all right?' he asked desperately. 'Tell me she's not badly hurt!'

'I don't think so,' Mandy said, quickly taking off her jacket and folding it into a pillow which she tucked under Casey's head. Casey was as white as a sheet and trembling a little, but her breathing was regular and her skin wasn't cold and clammy. As far as Mandy could tell, she wasn't in serious shock.

'What happened?' she asked in a dazed voice.

'You had an argument with a London taxi,' Mandy said, as calmly as she could, smoothing the hair back from Casey's face. 'I think the taxi won. Just lie still for now. Everything's going to be fine, don't you worry.'

'Why won't you let me get up off the sidewalk?' Casey asked feebly. 'I feel like an idiot lying here.' A small crowd was gathering around them by now. People were craning curiously to see who had been knocked over and if the victim was badly hurt.

'I think we should wait till your parents arrive,' Mandy said, pushing up the sleeve of Casey's sweatshirt so she could check her pulse wasn't racing too fast. 'James has gone to fetch them, so your dad'll be here any minute. He's a doctor,' she added, for the taxi driver's benefit.

'Well, I can see she's in good hands,' he replied thankfully, wiping a shaking hand across his forehead. 'Thanks, love. There was nothing I could do! She just stepped out in front of me!'

By now the Baxters were racing towards them, with James and the Hopes not far behind. Dr Baxter pushed his way through to Casey, then crouched down and began running his hands expertly over her body, talking to her all the while in a calm, gentle voice. Casey's mum knelt at her daughter's head, stroking her hair and trying very hard not to cry.

Quietly, Mandy stepped away. She'd done all she could, and she felt the Baxters needed some privacy. Her father obviously agreed, for he began to clear all the onlookers away. In a firm but pleasant voice, he asked everyone to give the family some space, telling them that everything was under control.

'Well done, love,' Mandy's mum said, giving her a comforting hug. 'Looks like you've done exactly the right thing.'

'Do you think she'll be OK?' James asked anxiously. Mandy nodded, not trusting herself to speak. She'd been fine when there was something to do, but now the shock of the accident was beginning to hit her. And then she remembered why Casey had been rushing across the street in the first place. The puppy! She looked over towards the side street, but it seemed deserted.

James followed her gaze. 'I'll go and take a quick look,' he said quietly. 'As long as there's nothing else I can do . . .'

'I think Casey's parents are the best people to look after her now,' Mandy said. 'Thanks, James.'

At last Dr Baxter began to help Casey up. 'She's fine, amazingly enough,' he said, when Casey was back on her feet, looking rather unsteady. 'No broken bones, and no internal injuries either – just a big shock to the system.'

Mandy let out her breath in relief, and everyone broke into smiles.

'Thank God!' said the taxi driver. 'I'm so sorry! She stepped right out in front of me,' he repeated to Casey's parents. 'Maybe she's not used to the traffic?'

'Hey! I live in New York,' Casey told him in a shaky voice. 'Of course I'm used to traffic! I'm just not used to it coming at me from the wrong direction, that's all.'

'We're going to get a nice hot cup of English tea, and then go straight back to Greenwich,' said Mrs Baxter, blowing her nose on a tissue. 'I think we've had enough excitement for one day.'

'I'll catch you later,' Casey said to Mandy as she was led away. 'We'll have a talk about you know what!'

Just then, Mandy saw James hurrying back

towards her. She raised her eyebrows at him in a silent question, although she could already tell from his disappointed expression that he had nothing to report. He just shook his head.

'And now I think *we* need a little chat, don't you?' Mandy's mother asked them both sternly. 'What were the three of you up to? Why was Casey running across the road like that?'

Mandy and James looked at each other, and then down at the ground. 'We spotted the puppy again when we were up in the tower,' Mandy said eventually. 'Casey saw it go down that side street, but now it's run off somewhere else.'

Mrs Hope sighed. 'Didn't you remember what I told you this morning?' she asked Mandy, a serious look in her green eyes. 'Look, of course we have to help an animal in trouble, but this puppy search seems to be turning into a wild-goose chase – and a dangerous one at that. Casey could have been killed just now!'

'London is a huge place,' Mr Hope added firmly. 'We can't possibly spend our whole holiday searching for a puppy that could be anywhere by now. It'd be like looking for a needle in a haystack! Somebody will find him and take him in to the police, I'm sure of it. So no more running around after lost dogs, OK? And certainly not now – it's time for lunch!'

'OK,' said Mandy, realising that she had to accept what her parents said – for the time being, at least. Inside her head, though, she made the puppy a silent promise. *Don't worry, we won't forget about you. We'll keep looking, if we can!*

When Mandy, James and her parents got back to The Crow's-Nest later that afternoon, Mac told them that Casey was resting in her room. The next morning, when the Baxters came down to breakfast, Mandy noticed Casey was walking a little stiffly. 'How are you?' she asked her straightaway. 'We've been so worried!'

'Oh, I really am fine,' Casey said. 'Just feeling a bit stupid for causing all this fuss and bother. And I have a bruise on my butt the size of a dinner plate.' She sat down next to Mandy and James, whose face had turned beetroot red. 'I don't suppose you saw any sign of the pup after all that commotion, did you?' she asked.

'No. I went down the side street to look, but he'd disappeared,' James replied, unfolding his napkin and trying to pretend he wasn't really blushing at all.

Mandy took a quick glance at her parents, sitting at the next table, and saw they were already chatting away to Dr and Mrs Baxter. 'Mum and Dad told us we should forget about the puppy for now,' she told Casey, lowering her voice. 'But I can't bear to think of him running around those busy streets. I wish he'd stayed in the Palace – he'd have been safer there.'

'I'm sure someone will catch him soon,' Casey said comfortingly, helping herself to orange juice from a big jug. 'He can't stay on the loose for ever.'

'Just so long as he doesn't get knocked over first,' Mandy worried, holding out her glass so Casey could fill it too. 'And what's he finding to eat? Where's he sleeping at night?'

'I bet he'll have found someone to look after him by now,' James answered reassuringly as he tucked into a bowlful of cereal. 'He's such a friendly little thing. Anyway, we'll be able to keep our eyes open for any sign of him when we go to the Royal Mews this morning. You are coming, aren't you, Casey?'

''fraid not,' Casey said. 'I'm still under house arrest. Dad says I've got to have a couple more quiet days before he'll let me back into the city.'

So after breakfast, they said goodbye to Casey and set off for the Royal Mews. Dorothy Hope, Mrs McFarlane and Eileen Davy were going to meet up with them at lunch-time in St James's Park, bringing a picnic Mac had prepared. 'Though I'm not sure a picnic will be grand enough for Mrs Ponsonby,' Mandy's gran told her. 'After a weekend in that wonderful hotel of hers, she's probably not prepared to sit on a rug in the park!'

Mandy stared up and down the street as she walked with James and her parents towards the Royal Mews at the side of Buckingham Palace. It was really no distance from where they'd been the day before – just a couple of roads away from Westminster Cathedral. But what busy roads they were! Mandy felt her heart sink as she watched the speeding traffic and the hundreds of people hurrying along the pavement. How could any puppy find its way safely around such a noisy, terrifying city?

'Wait till we get inside the stables,' James said

quietly to her. 'We may get a chance to ask if anyone spotted a puppy yesterday.'

It was a disappointing morning, though, as far as lost Labradors were concerned. Mandy and James both loved seeing the beautiful carriage horses, but none of the attendants had any news of a puppy having been reported around the Palace the day before. The stables were at the side of Buckingham Palace and backed on to the Palace grounds, so they kept their eyes open as they walked round. If the pup was still there, though, he didn't seem to want to be found.

After a couple of hours at the Royal Mews, they crossed the wide roads in front of the Palace and entered St James's Park to meet the others for lunch. Mandy began to feel more cheerful as she looked at the view. There was a lake in the middle of the park, sparkling in the sun, with a pretty bridge across it. Ducks and a couple of majestic swans were swimming to and fro underneath.

'It's like being back in the country!' she said to James.

'According to my guidebook there used to be a herd of cows kept here,' James replied. 'They'd milk them on the spot if anyone was thirsty, and charge a penny a glass. That was about three hundred years ago, though.'

Emily Hope laughed. 'What would we do without you and your guidebook, James!' she said, putting an arm round his shoulders and making him blush again.

As they headed across the grass towards the bandstand where they'd arranged to meet the others, Mandy heard a familiar voice booming out.

'I told the hotel manager that Pandora was extremely well-behaved,' Mrs Ponsonby was saying. 'After all, I trained her myself! There is no reason why she shouldn't be allowed into the dining-room. If anyone wants to complain, I'll soon put them right!'

Mrs Ponsonby was sitting in a deckchair next to Mandy's gran, in the shade of some trees near the bandstand. Miss Davy and Mrs McFarlane were with them too, helping to lay out Mac's picnic on a checked rug. Pandora was sitting on Mrs Ponsonby's lap, staring at the food and drooling.

'Hello, everyone,' Mandy said, dropping to her knees on the rug and suddenly realising she was starving. 'This picnic looks great!'

'Oh, hello, love!' her gran said, taking some cartons of juice out of the bag. She looked very relieved to see them. 'Have you had a good morning? I've been wondering when you were all going to get here.'

'Hello there, Mandy and James! And the rest of the family too, I see,' Mrs Ponsonby said, waving and smiling in a gracious manner. 'So nice to see familiar faces in the middle of London. Of course, when I meet the Queen, her face will look very familiar! But that's not quite the same, is it?' She laughed loudly.

Mandy passed round the paper plates and helped herself to an egg roll. She sat back on the rug, enjoying the fresh air and the warmth of the sun on her skin, listening to the others chatting quietly together. Gradually, though, she became aware of a strange snuffling sound above the background murmur. Pandora had jumped down from Mrs Ponsonby's lap and was advancing steadily towards some sausages, her little pink tongue hanging out of her mouth.

'Uh-oh, Pandora's decided it's time for her lunch too,' Mandy said, moving the plate to a corner of the rug out of the Peke's reach. She gave her a quick pat to make sure there were no hard feelings. Pandora shuffled back to her mistress's deckchair, looking rather put out.

'Never mind, my precious,' Mrs Ponsonby cooed, scooping her up again. 'You shall have some lovely chicken from Mummy's plate in a minute.'

Mandy and James exchanged glances. 'No wonder Pandora wants to eat our picnic,' Mandy whispered to James. 'You'd think Mrs Ponsonby would know better than to feed her like that.'

'So what have the rest of you been up to whilst we've been inspecting the Queen's horses?' her father said, munching on a cheese and tomato sandwich.

'We spent a most enjoyable morning at the Maritime Museum,' Miss Davy said. 'It was very interesting, and the staff were charming. Mr Pickard and Mr Bell came too.'

Suddenly Mandy froze, her roll halfway to her mouth. 'James!' she hissed. 'James! Look over there! And keep quiet!'

James had been about to pop open a packet of crisps. He put them down and stared around, trying to work out where Mandy was looking. And then his eyes widened as he caught sight of what she'd seen. From behind the large plane tree they were sitting under, an inquisitive little head was peeping out. A chocolate brown head, with soft floppy ears and shining dark eyes.

'There he is!' Mandy whispered excitedly, sitting up on her heels. 'That's our puppy!'

Six

As soon as he realised he'd been spotted, the little dog hid behind the tree again. Mandy held her breath, then released it slowly as she saw the Labrador's appealing face come back into view. Just like Pandora, he was staring hungrily at the sausages. Without realising it, Mandy had brought the plate much closer to him when she'd moved it away from the Pekinese.

'We've got to take this slowly,' she whispered to James. 'He seems much more jumpy now than when we saw him at the Palace.'

As casually as possible, she moved the plate of

sausages almost within the puppy's reach, in order to tempt him out. Trying not to startle him, she watched out of the corner of her eye as the little dog put his head on one side and licked his lips hungrily. He looked quite thin now, and there were muddy patches on his bedraggled brown coat. The puppy must have been having quite a tough time, and Mandy felt her heart melt. They had to make sure he was safe and properly looked after.

But she had forgotten Pandora. The Peke had obviously decided those sausages belonged to her, and she was watching them jealously. Growling softly in her throat, she waddled forward over the rug in hot pursuit of her escaping dinner. Unfortunately, the pup had chosen this very moment to pluck up his courage to dash out from the safety of the tree. He and Pandora came face to face with each other. The young Labrador was already taller than the fat little Pekinese, but there was no doubt who was top dog. Pandora bristled, her silky cream coat quivering with fury like an indignant powder puff, and let out a stream of shrill yaps.

'Pandora! My precious!' Mrs Ponsonby shrieked

in alarm, struggling up from her deckchair to find out what was the matter.

It was all too much for the poor Labrador puppy. He turned tail and fled across the grass towards the bandstand.

Mandy was already on her feet. 'Come on, James!' she called, tearing off after the puppy. 'We can't let him get away!'

Now that the pup was almost within their grasp, she was determined not to lose him again. She didn't want to alarm him even more by the chase, but they had to stop him once and for all. It was too dangerous for him to go running around on his own.

And then her eyes widened in horror. 'James!' she called, gasping for breath. 'Look where he's heading!'

The puppy was making straight for the huge ornamental gates at the side of the park, which lay wide open. Beyond them, traffic was speeding along the busy road and, if they weren't careful, they could drive the puppy straight into the path of the oncoming cars.

James waved and Mandy knew he'd seen the danger. He veered around in a circle to the left so that the puppy wouldn't be frightened by someone running just behind him. Then he swung back to try and head the puppy off before he could reach the gate. It was hopeless, though. The dog was too fast and they were both running out of steam – they just couldn't reach him in time.

Mandy could hardly bear to look as the pup headed straight for the inviting, open gates in front of him. A couple of people were strolling casually past, and Mandy yelled, 'Stop the puppy! Please, somebody, stop him!' But no one seemed to hear.

And then, just as the little Labrador was about to dash through the gates, a large group of tourists appeared. They stood in a long line along the pavement with their backs to the park, chatting excitedly and taking photographs of Buckingham Palace.

'Oh, thank goodness!' Mandy gasped to herself. The gateway was blocked.

The Labrador skidded as he turned around in confusion, all long legs and over-sized paws, and stood there, panting.

Mandy put on a final burst of speed. 'Got you!' she gasped, flinging her arms round the puppy and holding his heaving, wriggling body tight to her chest.

'Well, he's not in too bad shape, considering he's been on the run for a few days,' Adam Hope said, straightening up after examining the pup and giving him a pat on the head. 'And he *is* a he, too, if you see what I mean.'

'Are you sure he's OK?' Mandy said. She could detect a note of hesitation in her father's voice. 'Is anything wrong?'

'Well, I'm just a bit worried about his right ear,' Adam Hope replied. 'Do you see how he keeps shaking his head? And there's a lot of wax there. I think he might have some kind of irritation inside.'

'A grass seed perhaps?' Emily Hope said, looking over his shoulder. 'Difficult to tell without an auriscope, isn't it?'

'Is that serious?' Mandy asked, looking intently at the puppy.

'It could be,' her father replied. 'Grass seeds work their way down the dog's ear canal, you see, because of their pointed shape. If they end up next to the eardrum they can cause a lot of pain

or discomfort. We really need to get him to a vet right away so that ear can be properly examined with an auriscope, like your mother says.'

'Poor little thing.' Mandy said, stroking the pup gently. He was still quite wary but seemed much less frightened now, and lifted his head at the sound of her voice to lick her chin. 'What will happen to him if there *is* something stuck in his ear?' she asked.

'He'll have to have a general anaesthetic if there is an obstruction,' Mrs Hope replied. 'Just to keep him still while it's taken out.'

'But how do we know where the nearest vet is?' James asked anxiously. 'And what will happen to him after that?'

'Well, we could ring the RSPCA,' Adam Hope suggested. 'They'll probably treat him and then take him to a centre for stray dogs. They'll be able to find out there if he's been microchipped.'

'Oh, I hope he has,' Mandy said. She knew how much easier it was to reunite dogs with their owners if they'd had a specially coded microchip put into the scruff of their neck.

'Poor thing,' Mandy's gran said kindly, looking

at the timid little dog. 'It will all seem very strange to him.'

'Couldn't we just take him to the dogs' home ourselves?' Mandy asked her father. 'I'm sure they'll have a vet who could look at his ear. He's already becoming used to us, and it would be much less unsettling for him.'

'Do you know, I've always wanted to visit a dogs' home!' Eileen Davy said enthusiastically. 'Ever since I saw a television programme about one. May I come along with you?'

'All right, all right!' Mr Hope said, raising his hands in surrender. 'I can see when I'm outnumbered. Why don't the four of us take the pup in? I'm sure a taxi driver would know where the dogs' home is. Then your mother can have a nice long shop this afternoon with Gran.'

'I've got your number, Adam Hope!' Emily laughed. 'You'd do anything to get out of a shopping trip . . .'

'Casey's going to be so cross that she missed out on this,' Mandy said, as she sat with James and Miss Davy in the back of a black London taxi on their way to the dogs' home. The puppy dozed on the seat between them, his head resting on his paws. Occasionally he whimpered, and scratched his ear with his paw.

'We'll have to tell her all about it,' James said, stroking the puppy comfortingly. 'By the way, what do you think about Brownie as a name for the puppy?' he went on. 'Only for the moment, of course. He just reminds me so much of Blackie when he was little.'

'Hmm, maybe.' Mandy looked at the Labrador pup and tried to think of a way not to hurt James's feelings. 'Blackie is the perfect name for Blackie, of course. But I'm not quite so sure about Brownie . . .'

'Well, what about Bruno?' Miss Davy suggested. 'Would you say that had more of a ring to it?'

'Perfect!' James and Mandy decided together.

'Now don't go getting too attached to this puppy,' Adam Hope said, smiling at them from the pull-down seat opposite. 'We're taking him to the dogs' home and leaving him there so that his owner can claim him. And we're not bringing any other strays back with us to Welford, Mandy, no matter how appealing they are.'

'Don't worry, Dad,' Mandy sighed. 'I know the

rule.' There were too many animal patients at the Ark for the Hopes to adopt any more as pets. Mandy understood that, even though it was hard to accept sometimes.

The taxi soon drew up outside the dogs' home. Mr Hope paid the driver while James carried Bruno inside, holding him tightly, and Mandy followed on with Miss Davy. The puppy looked round nervously, trembling a little at the roar of the traffic.

'He's so much jumpier now than he was when we first saw him,' Mandy commented to Miss Davy. She'd already told her all about their first sighting of the pup at Buckingham Palace. 'It makes you wonder what's been happening to him over the past couple of days.'

'The poor creature must be terrified,' Miss Davy said sympathetically, holding an inner door open so James could carry Bruno into the reception area.

Ten minutes later, they were all sitting in a side room with Penny, who took charge of the dogs that people brought in. The door was firmly shut and Penny was giving the chocolate brown Labrador time to sniff around and get the feel of the place while she asked Mandy and James how they'd found him. They told her all about it, and Mr Hope told her about the puppy's ear problem too.

'I'll get Frank to have a look at him right away,' Penny said, completing the registration form.

After she had spoken to the centre's vet on the phone, she gazed thoughtfully at the puppy with her calm grey eyes. 'It certainly looks like he's come from a good home,' she commented. 'But I checked the register earlier this morning and I don't remember anyone having reported a missing Labrador. I'd have thought his owner would have been on to us or the police by now. Let me just check if he's been microchipped.' She ran a scanner over the scruff of Bruno's neck. 'No, nothing, I'm afraid,' she said, shaking her head.

'What if his owner never gets in touch?' James asked. 'What will happen to him then?'

'We'll keep him for seven days in the holding kennel,' Penny replied, taking a collar with a numbered identification disc and buckling it round Bruno's neck. 'If his owner hasn't turned up to claim him by then, he'll be moved over to the sale block so we can find him a new home.'

'Oh, Bruno!' Mandy said, unable to resist giving him another cuddle. 'How could anybody bear to part with you?'

'Don't worry,' Penny smiled. 'We'll take good care of him. If he isn't claimed, we'll make sure he goes to a new family who'll look after him properly. He won't be with us for long, I'm sure.' She snapped a lead on to the puppy's collar and stood up. 'Now then, Bruno, are you going to show me how well you walk to heel? Let's go and find your kennel! Then our vet can come and have a look at you. He's on his rounds now.'

'May we come too?' Mandy asked. 'Just to make sure he's OK?' She'd formed a real bond with this little puppy from the moment she'd first set eyes on him, and she was sure James felt the same. Saying goodbye was going to be very hard.

'Of course,' Penny said, looking at their sad faces. 'Why don't you all come, and then afterwards I can show you some of the other dogs? We've got cats too, though you might not have realised. They're much quieter!'

'That sounds like a good idea,' Adam Hope replied, putting a comforting arm round Mandy's shoulders. 'Let's go and see Bruno's new apartment!'

As they approached the kennel block, Mandy could hear the sound of barking. It rose to a crescendo when Penny opened the door and showed them in to a room lined on both sides with cages. They held about fifty dogs of all shapes and sizes. Some crowded up against the wire, yapping fit to burst, while others stayed in their baskets, looking out silently with nervous eyes. Bruno shrank back from the noise, so Penny scooped him up and carried him as she walked towards an empty kennel.

'These are the dogs that have been brought in today,' she said to James and Mandy over the din, pointing to the cages along one side of the room. 'The summer is our busiest time, I'm afraid. Some people don't bother to make proper arrangements for their pets when they go on holiday. They just turn them out on the street to fend for themselves.'

'They shouldn't be allowed to keep animals ever again,' Mandy said fiercely. Cruelty like that was something she would never understand or forgive. It made her blood boil.

Bruno was beginning to struggle in Penny's arms, so she handed him to Mandy and said, 'Would you like to put him in his basket? I think he's more used to you than he is to me.' She opened the door of the cage and stood back to let Mandy and James take Bruno inside. 'Don't worry, the vet will be here any minute,' she added reassuringly.

'We'll wait here,' Mr Hope said, as he and Miss Davy looked on. 'We don't want to crowd him.'

Mandy carefully settled the puppy into his basket. James knelt down beside her, giving Bruno a farewell pat before taking one last photograph for his collection.

'There you are, Bruno,' Mandy said encouragingly, arranging his blanket comfortably and trying to swallow the lump in her throat. She kissed the top of his satin-smooth head and whispered, 'It was nice knowing you. Goodbye, and good luck!'

Seven

'Now come on, you two,' Adam Hope said to James and Mandy, clapping an arm round each of their shoulders. 'There's no need to be upset. I bet Bruno's owner will come and collect him soon. He's in exactly the right place, and you've done the best for him you possibly could. So cheer up!'

'That's right,' Miss Davy added. 'And remember what Penny's told you – even if his owner doesn't turn up, there'll be plenty of people wanting to give Bruno a good home.'

'I suppose so,' Mandy said, blinking away her

tears. 'It's just strange leaving him here without knowing what's going to happen.'

'Well, you can always give me a ring in a few days' time to see if there's any news,' Penny said, leading them back out of the room. 'I'm sure we'll be able to rehome Bruno very quickly if we have to. Everyone wants a puppy, especially a pure-bred. It's a pity, really. So many of our older mongrels make brilliant family pets. Training an excitable puppy takes lots more time and patience.'

'That's true,' James said, and Mandy could tell exactly whom he was thinking of. 'I've got a black Labrador at home and he doesn't always do as he's told, even now he's fully grown!'

Penny took them over to what she called the 'sale block'. 'These are the dogs that are waiting to be rehomed,' she told them over a chorus of barks. 'We'll keep them for as long as it takes.'

'How could anyone choose between them?' Mandy wondered, as she passed cage after cage. German shepherds, terriers, greyhounds, lurchers – and more varieties of mixed-breed dogs than she could ever have imagined – rushed up to greet the visitors. Most of them were barking and wagging their tails furiously, as if pleading for a chance to show just what wonderful pets they would make.

'I'd like to take them all home – every one,' James said, as an eager mongrel tried to lick his fingers through the wire of the cage. 'I don't know what Blackie would think about it, though!'

'I sometimes think it's the dogs who pick their owners,' Penny said. 'You'll often find a dog will react to one particular person very strongly.' She smiled at the mongrel James was petting. 'This little fellow loves everyone, though,' she added.

'Do you ever get depressed, working here?' Mandy asked. She was finding the sight of so many abandoned dogs, desperate for a home, absolutely heartbreaking.

'Not often,' Penny replied. 'This is a very happy place, most of the time! Seeing an animal go off to a new home where you know he'll be loved makes all the difficult times worthwhile. But I do get angry at the state some of the poor things are in when they come to us. And it's sad to see some of our old-timers still here, month after month. Like Spike, for instance.'

She pointed to a large grey dog, curled up in

his basket. He opened one eye as they came up to the cage and lifted his head to watch them, but made no attempt to get up. 'Spike is the sweetest, gentlest creature you could imagine,' Penny explained. 'But as soon as people find out how old he is, they don't want to know.'

'I can't bear that kind of attitude,' Miss Davy said, and Mandy was surprised by the depth of feeling in her voice. 'It's the same with people. Once you've passed a certain age, it's as though you're not good for anything any more. But look at that lovely dog – he's got so much to offer.'

Spike raised his ears and looked at her. Then, slowly, he began to struggle stiffly to his feet.

'Now that's a surprise,' Penny said quietly. 'He doesn't usually bother to get up. It's as though he's given up hope of anyone taking an interest in him.'

Spike climbed out of the basket and padded towards them.

'Has he got some greyhound in him?' James asked. 'Look at those long legs! I bet he can run fast.'

Penny was too busy watching Spike to answer. He'd walked up to the cage door and was sitting there, staring intently at Eileen Davy and slowly

wagging the very tip of his tail. Then he barked –
just once – and turned to look at Penny. 'Well,
how about that?' she said in astonishment.

'Could he come out of the cage for a second?'
Mandy asked. 'It would be nice for Spike to have a
fuss made of him for once.' An idea was taking
shape in her head. Hadn't Penny said the dogs
sometimes chose their owners? From what she
could see, it certainly looked as though Spike had

chosen Miss Davy. Perhaps it would only take a little encouragement for her to fall for him, too.

'OK,' Penny said, already opening the cage door. 'I'm sure he'd love a bit of attention.'

Spike made a beeline straight for Miss Davy as soon as he was out of the cage. He pushed his head against her smart navy skirt, shedding a couple of pale hairs. Then he sat in front of her and solemnly offered a paw to shake.

'Oh, he's gorgeous, isn't he?' Mandy said. 'He's really taken to you, Miss Davy.'

'He definitely has,' Penny said. 'I've never seen him behave like this before!'

Eileen Davy held Spike's paw and gazed into his appealing eyes. 'I can guess exactly what's going through your mind, Mandy,' she said, in a voice that was rather softer than usual. 'But it's no use, I'm afraid. You can't just adopt a dog on a whim. It's a big commitment, and not one I'm ready to make just now.'

'Oh, Spike would be so happy—' Mandy began, but her father quietly interrupted her by laying his hands firmly on her shoulders.

'Mandy, Miss Davy is right,' he told her firmly. 'You can't force someone into a decision like this.

Not to mention all the practical difficulties! We're on holiday, remember, and we only came here to hand Bruno over. Now I think it's time for us to go.'

Mandy could hardly bear to watch as Penny led Spike back into his cage. She could feel his eyes burning into her back as they turned away, and hear his deep, urgent bark follow them out of the kennel block. *Don't leave me here!* he seemed to be calling. *Just give me a chance!*

They were all quiet on the journey back to The Crow's-Nest. Miss Davy stared out of the train window, lost in thought. Adam Hope fell asleep, and James read his guidebook. Mandy closed her eyes and let images from the dogs' home whirl around inside her head. She tried to think positively. Bruno would be well looked after there, she knew that, and if his owner didn't claim him, Penny would make sure he went to a good home. By the time the train had pulled into Greenwich station, she had convinced herself that Spike would also find a loving family soon. It was too painful to imagine him left at the centre for much longer.

They found Casey sitting in the back garden of The Crow's-Nest. 'You'll never guess what's happened!' Mandy told her. 'We've got the most amazing news!'

Casey laid down the book she'd been reading and squinted up at them from under her baseball cap. 'We've all been invited to tea at Buckingham Palace?' she said. 'The Millennium Dome has blown down in the wind? They've caught a shark in the Thames?'

'We found the puppy!' James announced triumphantly, sitting next to her on the bench. 'We were having a picnic in the park, and there he was!'

'That's great!' Casey exclaimed. 'But it's not so great that I wasn't there! Why didn't you come back and get me?'

'There just wasn't time for that,' Mandy smiled. 'We managed to catch him, and then we took him straight to the dogs' home. They're going to see if anyone claims him, and if not they'll find him a new home. We've given him a name, too – Bruno.'

'Oh, I wish I could take him back to the States!' Casey sighed. 'I feel like Bruno belongs to us, don't you? What was he like? Was he just as cute close-up?'

'He was adorable,' Mandy said. 'Wasn't he, James? It was so hard to part with him.' She fell silent, remembering how she'd felt as they walked away from the dogs' home. There had been two dogs she couldn't bear to leave behind, not just one.

'So what's been happening here?' James asked Casey. 'What have you done today?'

'Not much,' she replied with a huge yawn. 'Certainly nothing as exciting as that. We hung around here in the morning, and then we went shopping in the market this afternoon.'

'That's what Mum and Gran went to do, with Mrs McFarlane,' Mandy said, looking at her watch. 'Are they still not back?'

'Nope, nobody's here except for us and Mac,' Casey replied. 'He's in the kitchen, I think. But listen, I haven't told you the good news. Dad has passed me fit, so I can come to the Millennium Dome with you tomorrow.'

'That's great!' James said. 'I can't wait to see it.' Then a thoughtful look came over his face. 'Do you realise, Mandy,' he went on, 'we've only got two full days left in London? The time's going so quickly!'

'I know,' Mandy said. 'But then, on the other hand, I feel as if we've been here for ever.' She looked round the sunny garden. Patch, the little tortoiseshell cat, was stalking through some tall grasses in the border like a miniature tiger. And there, in the shade of an overhanging lilac tree, stood Sinbad's cage.

'Oh, Sinbad's here!' she said, going up to say hello. 'He's lost his voice all of a sudden.'

'You'll get a shock when you see him,' Casey warned, getting up to follow Mandy over.

Sinbad was sitting on the perch with his back towards them, but he turned around and whistled as they approached. 'Oh no!' Mandy gasped, horrified. 'Sinbad, what's happened to you?'

There were hardly any grey feathers left on his breast, and he'd even plucked away some of the down beneath so that bare skin showed through. He was a pathetic sight to behold – a bedraggled, scrappy-looking creature. 'Hello, Sinbad,' he squawked, as if he were trying to pretend nothing was wrong. Then he turned away again, as though too embarrassed to meet Mandy's eye.

'Mac found him like that in the dining-room this afternoon,' Casey said. 'He's really worried.'

James had come over to join them. 'Why on earth should Sinbad want to do that to himself?' he asked. 'It looks really sore!'

Mandy tried to remember what her mother had said. 'Apparently it's because he's under some kind of stress,' she said, thinking hard. 'But we've got no idea what's causing it.'

'You don't think Patch could be frightening him?' James asked. 'Cats do hunt birds, don't they? Perhaps he thinks she's after him.'

Casey shook her head. 'No, Mac told me they get on really well,' she said. 'Sinbad was here first, and he soon showed Patch who was boss. They're the best of friends now.'

Mandy remembered the first time they'd met Sinbad. It seemed ridiculous now to think that they'd been so frightened. Surely it couldn't just have been one parrot all by itself that had made them feel like that. What else was there? 'Come on!' she said suddenly. 'I think we need to go to the dining-room.'

'Why?' Casey asked as Mandy hurried them inside. 'What's there that we have to see in such a rush?'

'I'm not sure yet,' Mandy replied, throwing open

the door. 'But I think we need to get inside Sinbad's skin. There's something in this room that's making him uncomfortable, I'm sure of it. We felt it too, James, the first time we met him. We were scared, and it wasn't just because he was squawking at us.'

The three of them stared around the room. Then they all looked back at each other and said at exactly the same time, 'Daisy May!'

'She's lovely, isn't she?' Mac said, passing by on his way out of the kitchen with a tray of tea. 'I got her in the antiques market a couple of months ago.'

'No, you don't understand!' Mandy said, stumbling in her eagerness to get the words out. 'That's why Sinbad is so unhappy. He's on his own with her for most of the day, and he doesn't like it.'

Mac stared at her for a few seconds without speaking. 'Do you think so?' he said eventually. 'Come on, she's only a carving. I think she's beautiful.'

'She *is* beautiful,' Mandy replied eagerly, pulling him into the dining-room to face the figurehead. 'But, look – don't you think she's a bit threatening, too? Sinbad doesn't know she's not real. I think he's terrified of her.'

'We're certain that's it!' Casey added, speaking for all three of them.

'I suppose he does spend most of his time in here,' Mac said, putting the tray down on a side table and scratching his beard while he looked at Daisy May. He sighed. 'It was a big job getting her up on that wall. But if it'll help Sinbad, she'll just have to come down again.'

'But Sinbad's cage is on wheels,' James said. 'Why don't you put him somewhere else for the time being and see what happens?'

'Like the hall,' Mandy suggested, remembering the first time they'd seen Patch hiding behind the globe. 'There's so much to look at there, and people are coming and going all day. He'd get loads of attention!'

'Of course!' Mac said. 'I've just got so used to Sinbad being in this room that I've never considered moving him. But maybe he is a bit lonely here. And now I come to think of it, he did take a turn for the worse around the time that Daisy May arrived. I wonder if you could be right . . .'

'Oh, I hope we are,' Mandy said, thinking of the poor moth-eaten parrot out in the garden. 'We can't let Sinbad carry on hurting himself!'

Eight

Mandy woke up the next morning to sunlight streaming in through her curtains, and a strange sound floating up from downstairs. She quickly pulled some clothes on, trying not to disturb her gran who was still asleep, and crept out of the room.

'The sun has got his hat on,' Sinbad was squawking merrily, 'hip, hip, hip hooray! The sun has got his hat on and he's coming out today.' Mac had moved away a coatstand and put the parrot's cage in a corner of the hall, near a side window that looked out on to the street.

'Hello there, Sinbad,' she said, smiling at him through the bars. 'You're feeling very chirpy today, aren't you?'

'Hello, Sinbad!' the parrot replied, walking carefully down the perch to greet her. 'What a fine fellow!'

'Well, maybe not quite yet, but I'm sure you soon will be,' Mandy promised. 'I think you like it better here, don't you?'

'Oh, he's a different bird already,' Mac said, coming into the hall with a tea towel over his shoulder. 'This is the perfect place for him! It's not too draughty, and he can watch what's going on outside too. He's already made friends with the postman.'

'Mac! Mac!' Sinbad ordered as soon as he caught sight of his owner. 'Come here, boy.'

'That means he wants a tickle,' Mac told Mandy. 'I'm busy,' he called back to the parrot, but Sinbad just squawked his name again – even louder this time.

'OK, you old rascal,' Mac replied, putting down the towel and going over to open the cage door. Gently, he reached in to scratch the tiny feathers that overlapped each other like silvery chain mail on the top of Sinbad's head. 'I'm just kicking myself for not having thought of it before,' he went on. 'Sinbad's back to his old self, even if he is going to look a mess for a while longer. Thanks for solving the mystery, Mandy.'

'Oh, I'm just glad he seems to be better,' she said. 'Let's hope those feathers don't take too long to grow back.'

'You can get a cardboard collar from the vet's,' Emily Hope advised Mac, overhearing their conversation as she came down the stairs. 'Just to make sure he gets out of the habit of pecking himself.'

'I will,' Mac said, walking back towards the kitchen. 'Just as soon as I've finished the breakfasts. I thought we'd have waffles this morning, to celebrate.'

'We're going to miss Mac's cooking,' Mrs Hope said, putting an arm round Mandy's shoulders. 'But just look at this parrot! He certainly seems to like it here in the hall.'

Sinbad walked back down the perch and then suddenly picked his way up a rope at the side of the cage to swing upside down from the top, hooking his claws through the bars. 'Hello,

Sinbad,' he squawked again, looking cheekily back and making them both laugh.

'So, Mandy, there's nothing left for you to worry about,' her mother said, giving her a squeeze. 'Sinbad's going to get better and you found your runaway pup. Now you can really enjoy the last couple of days here.'

'I will!' Mandy replied, turning away from the cage. 'I wish we could have seen Bruno back together with his owner, but at least we know he's safe.'

'And we're going to visit the Dome today,' her mother reminded her. 'I can't wait to see what it's like inside!'

A couple of hours later, full of waffles and maple syrup, everyone wandered down the street to catch a bus that would take them the short distance to the Dome.

'Are Walter and Ernie coming?' Mandy asked her grandmother as they waited at the bus stop. 'We've hardly seen them this holiday.'

'Yes, we're going to meet them outside the Dome at ten, along with Mrs McFarlane,' her gran replied. 'I rang the pub last night to arrange it.'

She laughed. 'I think they've had enough of city life. Ernie said he would never have guessed how noisy London was.'

'D'you know, I'm looking forward to going back too,' Casey confided to Mandy and James. 'We've had a great time here, and I'm so glad I've met you both, but there's no place like home, is there?'

'No, there isn't,' Mandy agreed, thinking rather wistfully about Animal Ark. She looked around the bustling street, thronging with traffic and overlooked by terraced houses and blocks of flats. How different her life would have been if she'd been adopted by a family who lived in the city! It made her head spin just thinking about it.

Then a huddled figure sitting in a doorway near the bus stop caught her eye. 'Buy a magazine and help the homeless?' the man asked, waving a copy in her direction.

'Sure,' Mandy said, fumbling for her purse. She still had most of her spending money left over and, besides, they'd just been talking about how much they were all looking forward to going home. Here was someone who didn't have a home at all and Mandy wanted to help.

'Thanks, love,' said the man, handing over the

magazine. 'Have a nice day! Where are you off to?'

'We're going to the Millennium Dome,' Mandy said. 'Oh, can I say hello to your dog?' A bright-looking little terrier was sleeping on a blanket at the man's feet.

'Course you can,' he replied, tucking Mandy's pound coin away in his pocket. 'She won't bite. Her name's Lucy, if you want to introduce yourself. And I'm Joe.'

'Hello, Lucy,' Mandy said solemnly, patting the dog's head. 'My name's Mandy. It's nice to meet you.'

James and Casey came over to join them, and they each bought a magazine too. Lucy wagged her stumpy tail ten to the dozen, delighted with all the attention she was getting.

'Oh, she's gorgeous!' Casey said to Joe. 'If she's not careful, she'll wag that tail right off!'

'How long have you had her?' Mandy asked.

'I found her in a dustbin last year,' Joe said, stroking his dog with a grimy hand. 'Someone had dumped her, along with the rubbish. But I took her to the animal hospital and she's fine now. We're company for each other, Lucy and me.

'I wouldn't be without her for the world.'

'It can't be easy to look after her sometimes,' James said shyly. 'I mean, if she's ill or anything.'

'We get by,' Joe said. 'She's had all her jabs and I take her back to the animal hospital if she gets any problems. It's easier in the summer but we make it through the winter as best we can. She's a good little hot-water bottle, that's for sure!' He looked over to the bus stop. 'Oh, it looks like that's your bus. Better not miss it!'

Mandy's parents were calling them over. 'Coming!' Mandy shouted back. She looked at the money in her purse. Suddenly the idea of spending it on tacky plastic souvenirs didn't seem such a good one. 'Here,' she said, giving Joe a five-pound note. 'Can you put this towards a coat for Lucy? She might be glad of one when it gets colder.'

'Well, thanks very much,' said Joe, delighted. His smile grew even broader when James and Casey added their own money to the collection. 'She'll have the warmest coat in London this winter,' he promised, holding Lucy up and waving goodbye as they got on the bus. 'Come and visit again and you'll see!'

They waved back out of the window as the bus pulled away. 'It's great to come across someone who really cares about their dog,' James commented, as Joe and Lucy grew smaller in the distance. 'Especially after all those poor strays we saw yesterday.'

'I was just thinking exactly the same,' Mandy agreed. 'Lucy might not have regular meals or a warm bed, but I'd say she was a lot better off than Spike. She's got someone who loves her, and that's more important than anything.'

'Look, there's the Dome!' Mandy's dad said as

the white mushroom shape, familiar from so many photographs, came into view. But Mandy was still thinking about Spike, though. She hoped he and Bruno would soon have owners to love them as much as Joe obviously loved Lucy. But, somehow, she wasn't convinced.

Nine

'Now what are we going to do on our last day in London?' Adam Hope asked, looking round the breakfast table the following morning.

'It's a pity the weather's not a bit better,' said Mandy's gran, gazing out at the cloudy sky. 'Mrs Ponsonby's got her famous garden party this afternoon. I hope her new hat doesn't get wet, or we'll never hear the end of it!'

'Why don't we take a bus trip round London?' James suggested. 'I noticed special sightseeing buses at the station. You can get on and off them wherever you like, and they take you to all the famous places.' Suddenly, realising that everyone's eyes were on him, he stopped and looked rather embarrassed. 'But I don't mind if no one else wants to,' he said. 'It's just an idea.'

'Well, I think it's a very good one,' Emily Hope said, draining her cup of tea. 'We had such a busy time yesterday. Watching the world go by from a seat on the bus is just what I feel like doing!'

'Me too,' Mandy said. 'Why don't we all go? I'm sure the Baxters would like to come, and we *have* to spend our last day with Casey. We could get Walter and Ernie along, too, and Miss Davy and Mrs McFarlane. Then we could all go out for a meal this evening. What do you say, Gran?'

'I'd say you two had better plan next year's trip!' laughed her grandmother. 'It all sounds perfect, dear. I'll give Walter and Ernie a ring – I'm sure they'd love to come.'

It didn't seem long before everyone was sitting upstairs on the open top deck of a sightseeing bus. The sun was just breaking through the clouds as they pulled away to start the tour.

'Would you just look at that traffic!' Ernie said, looking down at the road as they approached

Trafalgar Square. 'Those cars are packed solid!'

'Where are we now?' Casey asked James. 'I didn't hear what the guide said. What's that big pillar coming up?'

'That's Nelson's Column,' James replied. 'This is one of the places I thought we could stop off at for a while. I really want to take some photos of those big stone lions at the bottom.'

'Sounds good to me,' Mandy said, getting up from her seat as the bus drew to a halt. 'Who's coming?'

It turned out that everyone wanted to see the lions at the foot of Nelson's Column and have a wander round Trafalgar Square. There were flocks of pigeons everywhere and even a couple of seagulls, wheeling round the fountains. After James had taken a few shots, he decided to get everyone together for a group picture. 'Mr Pickard and Mr Bell, could you stand at the back,' he called. 'Then Mandy and Casey in the middle, please, with everyone else sort of gathered around.'

'Do you want my cap on or off?' Walter Pickard called out obligingly.

'Off, I think,' James replied from behind the

camera. But then, instead of taking the photo, he lowered his camera and stood peering at something behind them.

'Oh, come on, James!' Mandy called impatiently. 'We've been standing here for ever. Hurry up and take the picture so I can go and feed the pigeons!'

But James just carried on standing still, holding the camera loosely by his side and staring at the fountain behind them on the other side of the square. 'I don't believe it!' he said, pointing towards it.

Mandy turned to look. She rubbed her eyes and looked again. Surely, it couldn't be? But there, splashing happily around in the fountain, was a mischievous little brown Labrador puppy. 'Bruno!' she gasped in amazement. 'But that's impossible!'

'Now this is someone I have to meet!' Casey said, striding towards the fountain. 'After all, I missed out last time.'

'Careful, Casey!' Mandy warned, rushing along after her. 'He's quite nervous and he could easily run out into the road. There are cars everywhere!'

The puppy was romping through the shallow
water, sending up showers of spray and drenching
a small group of tourists that had gathered to
watch him play. They didn't seem to mind,
though. Cameras were clicking and everyone was
smiling at the adorable little dog.

'Here, boy!' Casey whistled. 'Come here,
Bruno.'

To Mandy's surprise, the puppy splashed
obediently towards her, pink tongue hanging out
of one side of his mouth as he bounded over.

'Well, you're not nervous with me, are you?' Casey said, as she patted him. 'You are *so* cute! I don't even mind the fact you're making me wet through.'

Mandy stared at the Labrador pup, still hardly able to take in what she was seeing. There were a few muddy patches on his damp coat, but he seemed to be in good spirits and otherwise unhurt.

'You should keep your dog on a lead,' an elderly woman said severely to Mandy, turning back to look disapprovingly at Casey over the top of her glasses. 'He could cause a nasty accident.'

'He's not exactly our dog,' Mandy began, unable to take her eyes off the puppy. Casey was holding him securely while he shook himself, sending silver droplets of water flying through the air. By now, Mandy's parents and the Baxters had come over, followed by Miss Davy and the others.

'Pass me your tie, please, Dad,' Casey asked her father. 'We need an emergency lead here.'

'What on earth is this little fellow doing here?' Mr Hope exclaimed. 'The last time we saw him, he was safely in his cage at the dogs' home!' He gave the puppy a quick look over. 'Well, his ear seems fine now,' he said. 'That's something, I suppose.'

'We'll have to tell the dogs' home we've found him again,' Mandy said, crouching down to have a good look at Bruno as he sat by Casey's feet, the tip of his tail wagging furiously. 'He must have escaped somehow.'

'But how has he found his way here?' James wondered. 'Think of all the traffic he's had to get through.'

'Well, however he managed it, I think we need to take him back to the home right away, don't you?' Miss Davy said. 'They must be very worried about him going missing. Come on, this time it's my turn to pay for the taxi.' And she started walking towards the road to look for one.

'What about our sightseeing trip?' Ernie said. 'There's another bus stopped over there – we could have caught it.'

'Why don't the rest of you go on without us?' Adam Hope replied. 'Let's arrange to meet up again at that café in St James's Park for lunch. About one o'clock?'

'Well, if you're sure you don't mind taking care of our daughter,' said Dr Baxter. 'And Casey, that's my favourite tie. I want it back again!'

Miss Davy soon managed to hail a taxi, and everyone went over towards it. The little pup bounded along at Casey's side, quite happy to come along with them. Miss Davy held open the door and he hopped in and sat on the back seat as though he'd been riding in taxis all his life.

The taxi driver muttered something grumpily. 'You'll have to squash up,' he said over his shoulder in a louder voice. 'Five passengers is the most I'm allowed to take, and that's not counting any dogs. And I hope he's not making a mess of my upholstery.'

'Come on, Bruno,' Mandy said, scooping him on to her lap. 'You'd better sit here with me.' She laid her cheek against his smooth brown head and added, 'No more running off on your own now – OK?'

'There's something really strange about this,' Mandy said, as they waited for Penny to meet them in the reception area at the dogs' home. She took another long look at the puppy, who was busy winding Dr Baxter's best tie into knots as he explored an interesting corner behind the chair.

'You're telling me!' James replied. 'I still can't believe Bruno managed to get all the way from here to Trafalgar Square. It's on the other side of the river!'

'And without getting run over or caught,' said Mandy's father. 'That really is incredible. Maybe someone befriended him, but then why didn't they take him into a police station?'

'There's something else, though,' Mandy went on. 'He seems so different now – much more confident and bouncy. Look how easy it was to catch him. He got really spooked when we went after him on Monday.' She clicked her fingers and the pup immediately came running up to sniff them. 'See what I mean?' she said.

'It's because I'm here, of course,' Casey joked, giving the pup a cuddle. 'I've got a way with dogs. If I'd been around last time, you wouldn't have had any problems.'

Before Mandy could think of a witty reply, Penny appeared. 'Well, hello again,' she said. 'Have you come to visit Bruno? He's still feeling pretty miserable, I'm afraid.'

'What do you mean?' James replied. He pointed towards the puppy, who had started to run in circles around Casey's feet. 'Look! Bruno's here with us.'

Penny gave a start as soon as she caught sight of the little dog. 'But that's impossible!' she exclaimed. 'I don't believe it!'

'Neither could we,' Mandy said. 'We found him splashing around in the fountain in Trafalgar Square just now. Didn't you know he'd gone missing?'

'He isn't missing, though!' Penny said. 'I've just walked past Bruno, asleep in his cage in the holding block. You were right, by the way – he did have a grass seed in his ear. We got it out just in time.' She gave the puppy a pat, looking intently at him. 'Well,' she said, smiling up at their astonished faces, 'this little fellow's just as gorgeous, but he's not our Bruno.'

They all stared at her for a moment, unable to take in this amazing piece of news.

'So that's why you thought there was something different about him, Mandy,' said Adam Hope. 'He's another dog altogether!'

'Which means there are two lost puppies,' Mandy said slowly. 'And we've found both of them.'

The pup began to wind his makeshift lead around Casey's legs, worrying away at it with sharp white teeth. 'Hold on there, fella,' she said. 'My dad's going to kill me if you eat his tie.'

'I think you'd better come with me and we'll check him in,' Penny said, bending down to give the puppy a quick examination. 'Then we can give him a proper collar and his own number. It'll be hard to tell him and Bruno apart.'

'They must be from the same litter, don't you think?' Mandy said, crouching down beside her. 'Same age, same colouring. And Trafalgar Square isn't that far from St James's Park – where we picked up Bruno.'

'So no one's reported losing any Labrador puppies yet?' Miss Davy asked.

'No, they haven't,' Penny replied, giving the puppy a final stroke and straightening up. 'I really can't understand it. These two have obviously come from a good home, and they're so appealing. I'd have thought they'd have been claimed straight away, but no one's contacted the police or the RSPCA, or any of the local vets. It's very strange.'

It certainly is, Mandy thought. *If those two puppies*

belonged to me, I wouldn't let them out of my sight!

'I'll just check this pup in and then we can take him to see Bruno,' Penny went on. 'Come with me and we'll get the forms filled out. I'm sure you remember the process from last time!'

'Perhaps we should call him Nelson for the time being,' James suggested as they followed Penny into the main part of the home. 'After all, we were standing by Nelson's Column when we saw him. Nelson and Bruno – what do you think?'

'I think that sounds great,' Mandy replied, looking at the bouncy little pup as he scampered along beside them, nose to the ground in search of interesting smells. 'Nelson really suits him somehow.'

'Nelson it is, then,' Casey said, giving James a pat on the back.

'Who knows, maybe their owner will turn up soon and we'll find out what their real names are,' Penny added over her shoulder.

'Oh, I hope so,' Mandy sighed. She couldn't shake off the feeling that someone, somewhere, must be desperate to find both Nelson and his brother.

* * *

'Well, those two are certainly happy to see each other!' Casey commented as they watched the two puppies playing together. As soon as Bruno had caught sight of Nelson, he'd rushed up to the cage door and thrown himself against it, whining and barking excitedly. Now the two of them were tearing round the kennel, wrestling each other to the ground with lots of playful nips and growls. James took photo after photo until he ran out of Polaroid film.

'Bruno'll be so much happier to have some company,' Mandy said. 'Leaving him behind doesn't feel as bad now Nelson's with him.'

'I promise I'll give you a ring and tell you what happens to them,' Penny said as she bolted the cage door. 'When are you going home?'

'Tomorrow morning,' Mandy said. 'And Casey and her parents are leaving the day after that.' She took one long last look at the two puppies, now curled up together on the blanket. 'Oh, I hope they'll be OK!'

'We'll look after them, don't you worry,' Penny reassured her as they began to walk away.

'Actually, there is just one more thing,' Miss Davy said, and something about the tone of her voice made everyone stop and look at her. 'I don't want to hold you all up,' she went on, taking a deep breath, 'but I would like to see Spike again before we go.'

'Oh, Miss Davy!' Mandy breathed, hardly daring to hope. 'You don't mean—'

'Yes, I do,' Eileen Davy said firmly. She turned to Penny. 'I've been thinking this over very carefully, and I *would* like to offer him a home. If you think mine would be suitable, that is.'

Before Penny could say anything in reply, Mandy had thrown her arms round Miss Davy and given her a big hug. 'Oh, that's wonderful!' she cried. 'He'll be so happy with you, I know he will! We'll help you walk him, and Mum and Dad can look after him in the surgery if he needs anything—'

'Steady on, Mandy!' Miss Davy said, though her eyes were shining and she didn't look at all cross. 'I'm sure there are a lot of questions Penny needs to ask. I haven't been approved yet! But I haven't been able to get that dear old dog out of my mind, and coming back here for the second time seems like fate. I think I'm meant to have him.'

Penny was smiling too. 'You're right, there are a lot of things we need to discuss,' she said. 'But

I'm delighted you feel this way, and Spike will be too. I'm sure we can work it all out!'

'That's marvellous news, Eileen,' Mr Hope said, and soon everyone was patting Miss Davy on the back and shaking her hand.

'Even if everything goes smoothly, you won't be able to take him away just yet, I'm afraid,' Penny warned. 'But we can certainly start the ball rolling now. Come back to my room for a moment and we'll get going on the forms.'

'Why don't we wait for you in the café here?' Mandy's dad suggested. 'I could do with a cup of tea after all this excitement!'

They were just finishing their drinks by the time Miss Davy came back. She looked as neat and composed as usual but, underneath, Mandy could tell she was feeling very emotional. 'Well, someone from the home is going to visit me next week,' she informed them. 'If all goes well, I could have Spike with me in Welford by the end of the month. There are my hens to consider, of course, but Penny tells me he's much too good to chase them. He really is the most delightful dog!'

'And we'd never have met him if it wasn't for

the puppies,' Mandy said. 'Oh, Miss Davy, you are lucky!' She turned to her father, determined to try one question out on him, although she already had a very good idea what the answer would be.

'Dad,' she began, 'if the puppies' owner doesn't turn up, do you think there's any way . . .'

'No, Mandy, I'm sorry,' her father replied firmly. 'Hold it right there. They're beautiful dogs, but there's no way we can take them on. I know it seems hard, but we just can't—'

'Oh, thank goodness I caught you before you left!' Penny came bursting through the swing doors and rushed up to their table. She sank down on a chair next to them to catch her breath. 'I've just taken a call from a woman who's lost her puppies,' she went on. 'They're Labradors – chocolate-coloured ones. I think we've found Nelson and Bruno's owner! She's on her way over here now, and she wants to talk to you. Can you wait?'

Ten

'Oh, please can we stay here a little longer?' Mandy begged her father. 'I couldn't bear not to know whether Nelson and Bruno really have been claimed!'

'I should think so,' Adam Hope replied. 'We've come this far, so we may as well find out how the story ends.' He looked at his watch and added, 'We might be a bit late meeting the others for lunch, but I'm sure they won't mind waiting.'

'Don't worry,' said Miss Davy, getting to her feet. 'I'll go back to the park and let them know you've been delayed. To be honest, I want to share my good news with everyone. You can tell me later what happens with the puppies.'

'Their owner – if she really is their owner – doesn't live far away,' Penny said, after Miss Davy had left. 'It won't take her very long to get here. Apparently she's some famous writer, though I hadn't heard of her. Jane, our switchboard operator, recognised the name.' She looked down at the notepad she was holding. 'Where is it now? Yes, here we are: Laura Dawson.'

'*What?*' James and Mandy exclaimed together. 'Laura Dawson? Not *the* Laura Dawson?'

'Looks like it,' Penny said, grinning at their startled faces. 'Jane says her son's a big fan. He's got all the books she's ever written.'

'You know Laura Dawson!' Mandy said excitedly, turning to Casey. 'She's the author of all those fantastic animal stories – the *Sweetwater Sanctuary* series and the *Running Wild* books, and loads of others. You're reading one of hers at the moment. I saw you, in the garden the other day.'

'Of course!' Casey said. 'So that's why her name sounded familiar. Wow! It's such a great story, and I'm going to meet the person who wrote it! Now

I really do have something to tell everyone back home.'

Mandy stared into the distance. 'To think, we might actually have rescued Laura Dawson's puppies,' she said in a faraway voice. 'I can't believe it.'

'Well, it sounds like she could do with some advice on looking after them,' said Emily Hope. 'Brilliant writer or not.'

'I agree,' Penny said. 'There are a few things we need to ask Laura Dawson when she arrives. If Nelson and Bruno do belong to her, she's lucky to be getting them back in one piece.'

'There has to be some explanation,' Mandy said stubbornly. Laura Dawson was her favourite author. She wrote so beautifully about animals – surely she would know how to take care of her own?

Fifteen minutes later, a slim, anxious-looking woman with a large bag slung over one shoulder came rushing into the dogs' home. The swing doors banged noisily behind her. James, Casey, Mr Hope and Mandy had moved over from the café to wait for Laura Dawson in the reception area, and Mandy realised immediately that the famous writer had just arrived. She'd once seen her photograph on a poster in a bookshop.

'My name is Laura Dawson,' the woman said, hurrying up to the reception desk. 'I think you may have my puppies.'

Mandy felt James nudge her side urgently. 'There she is!' he hissed. 'Go on, say something!'

'Take a seat and someone will be with you shortly,' the receptionist answered calmly, picking up her phone.

Laura Dawson walked towards them. Mandy had a quick impression of piercing blue eyes, fair skin and dark wavy hair gathered back into a loose plait. 'Um, Ms Dawson,' she began, standing up. 'We, er, found your puppies and brought them here. If they are yours, that is. I'm Mandy Hope, and these are my friends James and Casey, and my father—'

'Oh, Mandy, I'm so glad to meet you!' Laura Dawson said. She smiled hello at all of them and then took Mandy's hand in her own for a moment. 'I don't know how to thank you enough, really I don't. And please, do call me Laura. I've been out of my mind with worry—'

'Why didn't you report them missing?' Mandy blurted out. 'We can't understand why no one's come for them till now.'

'Mandy!' James exclaimed, looking horrified that she should dare to say such a thing – to Laura Dawson, of all people.

'I'm sorry,' Mandy went on. 'It's just that anything could have happened to the puppies, running round London on their own. It's a miracle they weren't run over.'

'But I only found out they were lost an hour ago!' Laura Dawson exclaimed, rubbing a hand anxiously across her forehead. 'I came as soon as I could.'

Mandy stared at her uncertainly. How could that possibly be true? They'd first seen Bruno at Buckingham Palace on Saturday – five days ago.

Penny came into the reception area. 'You must be Ms Dawson,' she said, sounding very formal and just a little bit disapproving. 'Would you like to come with me now and I'll take you to the puppies?'

'Yes, of course!' Laura said, jumping to her feet. 'Oh, I do hope they're mine – they've just got to be! You must let me explain—'

'Why don't we talk on the way over?' Penny said, holding the door open. 'I'm sure you'd like to see the dogs as soon as possible.'

'Can everybody else come along?' Laura asked. 'I've got so many questions to ask.'

'I'll stay and wait for you here,' Adam Hope volunteered. 'It might be better not to have too many people crowding around.'

Penny led the way down the corridor and Mandy, James and Casey followed on behind with Laura Dawson.

'How come you've only just discovered the puppies had strayed?' Mandy asked her as they walked off. Laura was so warm and friendly, she didn't feel intimidated by her at all.

'Because I've been away on a publicity tour and didn't get back 'til this morning,' Ms Dawson replied, hoisting up her enormous bag as it slid down one shoulder. 'I've been giving interviews about my new series and signing copies – all that commotion.'

'*Every Living Thing*, you mean?' James asked, his eyes shining excitely behind his glasses. 'I've got the first book at home. It's brilliant!'

'I'm glad you like it,' Laura Dawson replied, with

a quick smile. 'Well, I went away on Saturday and left the dogs at home with my housekeeper. Apparently, she'd given them a bath and taken their collars off.' She patted her bag and added, 'I've brought them with me, and their leads too. Oh, I do so hope these really are my puppies!' She paused and bit her lip before carrying on. 'Anyway, they were running around the garden to dry off in the sun, and the side gate had been left open. That must have been how they escaped.'

'And your housekeeper didn't let you know?' Casey asked. 'Or report it to the police?'

'She thought she could find them on her own before I got back, and then I'd never need to know,' Laura replied. 'She kept ringing the police to see if anyone had brought them in, but wouldn't leave her details in case I got to hear of it. And she didn't think to contact the dogs' home, I'm afraid.'

'Well, here we are,' Penny said as she opened the door to the holding block. 'Let's hope the story has a happy ending.' Suddenly, the air exploded into a frenzy of barks and whines as the dogs inside greeted their visitors.

'We've called them Nelson and Bruno,' Penny

went on, walking towards the puppies' cage, 'though you may be able to tell us what their real names are.'

Laura Dawson followed Penny. Mandy realised she could hardly bear to look at the cage, in case she'd discover the puppies inside belonged to someone else. Nelson had rushed up to the wire and was standing there, wagging his tail, while Bruno hung back behind him. As soon as they saw Laura, they burst into high-pitched, excited barks, throwing themselves against the door in their eagerness to get at her.

'Oh, yes!' she exclaimed, crouching down to their level. 'These are mine – George and Henry! Thank goodness they're safe!' Penny opened the cage door and the two little dogs rushed out into Laura's waiting arms, nearly knocking her over in their excitement. 'Stop it! Enough!' she laughed, as they tried to lick every inch of her face.

'That's wonderful!' Mandy said, swapping delighted smiles with James and Casey as they watched the happy reunion. There could be no doubt at all that these were Laura Dawson's puppies, and that they were as overjoyed to see her as she was to find them.

'So where's Princess?' Laura asked, looking up at Penny as the two dogs tumbled over each other in her lap. 'Is this cage too small for three? Are you keeping her somewhere else?'

'I'm sorry?' Penny said blankly. 'Who's Princess? These are the only Labrador puppies we have.'

Mandy felt a cold chill sink into her stomach. She saw the joy in Laura's face slowly fade as she stammered, 'But I have three dogs – George, Henry and Princess. Didn't you find them all together?'

'No, I'm afraid we didn't,' Mandy replied, kneeling down beside Laura and trying to calm the puppies while she explained. 'We saw one of the pups at Buckingham Palace first, on Saturday, and then we spotted one in Victoria Street the next day. But we only managed to catch this fellow on Monday, in St James's Park. He's the one we called Bruno.' And she picked out the more timid of the two pups.

'That's Henry,' Laura said, hugging him to her. 'So he was all on his own?'

'Yes! We didn't find his brother until this morning, in Trafalgar Square,' Mandy said. 'At first, we thought he must have been Bruno – I mean, Henry – who'd escaped from the dogs' home. We didn't realise there were two puppies.'

'And we had no idea there were three!' James put in. 'Where on earth could Princess be?'

'That's what we'll have to work out,' Mandy said determinedly. 'We've found George and Henry – now we have to find their sister!'

'The thing is, we don't know which puppy we saw where,' Mandy said, looking at the circle of intent faces round the table. The two Labrador pups had been checked out of the dogs' home and now everyone was back in the café, trying to decide what to do next. Laura Dawson was sipping a cup of tea while Henry sat as close to her as he possibly could, resting his head on her lap. George lay on his back under the table, looking blissfully happy as James scratched his tummy.

'The puppies are so alike!' Mandy went on. 'It could have been Princess we saw at Buckingham Palace or in Victoria Street, or maybe we haven't seen her at all. We just don't know!'

'Let's go through everything once again,' Casey

suggested. She turned to Laura. 'The pups all escaped from your house on Saturday morning. And that's in Victoria Square, right? Just behind the Palace?'

'That's right,' Laura answered distractedly. 'And now it's Wednesday! It's awful to think of them being lost for all this time.'

'Well, at least these two turned up safe and sound in the end,' Mr Hope said encouragingly. 'Let's hope Princess will too.'

'Perhaps we should try and work out whether we might have seen her anywhere,' Mandy said. 'Is there anything unusual about her? Any distinguishing marks?'

Laura shook her head, as if trying to clear it. 'She's a little bit smaller than her brothers,' she said, stroking Henry's ear. 'But they do look very similar, chocolate brown all over.' She thought for another few seconds and then said slowly, 'There is one thing, I suppose. Princess has a real Labrador grin. You know how they seem to smile when they're pleased to see you? Well, she could smile for England.'

'My photos!' James exclaimed, reaching inside his rucksack. 'Of course! Why didn't I think of that before?' He pulled out a sheaf of pictures and started leafing through them. 'There!' he said, pulling out one of the early prints. 'Do you recognise Princess? Could this be her?'

Laura Dawson fumbled in her bag and came out with a pair of gold-rimmed glasses. She put them on and looked intently at the photo, while Mandy craned over her shoulder to see it too. The little Labrador puppy gazed back out of the photograph at them, head to one side and one ear raised enquiringly. Mandy could just make out the tip of a pink tongue, and the beginnings of a doggy smile.

'That's Princess!' Laura said delightedly. 'No doubt about it – there she is.' She took off her glasses and smiled as she put them back in her bag. 'At Buckingham Palace, of all places!'

'Well, she has the right name for it,' Adam Hope said, tucking into his sandwich. 'But that photo was taken a few days ago. I wonder where she is now?'

'She might still be there,' Mandy suggested. She thought back to when they'd first seen the pup, bounding through the archway below the balcony and on into the grounds beyond. 'After all,

Buckingham Palace probably seems like paradise to her. According to James's guidebook there are gardens at the back, with a lake.'

'And these puppies do seem very adventurous,' James added. 'Remember where we found the other two.'

'It's not exactly the easiest place to search though, is it?' Casey said, draining her can of lemonade. 'We can't just go up to the gate and say, "Excuse me, Your Majesty, but we think our dog's in your garden. Can we have a look for her?"'

'No, we can't,' Mandy said, thinking hard. 'But somebody we know is going to Buckingham Palace this afternoon, isn't she?'

'Mrs Ponsonby!' James said, with a broad smile. 'Of course!'

'Look, I don't want to pour cold water on your brilliant idea, Mandy,' said her father, 'but we don't even know what time Mrs Ponsonby's meant to be at Buckingham Palace. By the time we get over there, she may well have gone inside.'

'Then I think we should wait for her to come out,' Mandy said. 'Oh, I know there's only a slim chance of finding Princess there, but it's worth a try, isn't it? And there's no way we could get inside the Palace ourselves.'

'Well, we should be getting back to St James's Park now,' Mr Hope said, looking at his watch again. 'The others must be getting tired of waiting for us.'

'I wish I could give you a lift,' said Laura, standing up and untangling the puppies' leads. They sprang to their feet, looking up at her expectantly as though they were eager to get home. 'I couldn't possibly fit you all in my car, though.' Then, fumbling in her bag, she said rather awkwardly, 'I would like to offer you a reward for all the trouble you've taken. Please, would you accept a token of my gratitude?'

'Oh, no! Please don't,' Mandy said, and saw her father was shaking his head too. 'It's been enough of a reward meeting you – and George and Henry, of course!'

'Well then, at least let me pay for your taxi fares,' Laura said, pressing a note into Mr Hope's hand, despite all his protests. 'I'd better get the puppies home now,' she went on, 'but after I've made sure they're OK, why don't I come back and meet you outside the Palace? There must be something I can do to help.'

'Fine,' Mandy said. 'We'll be there, however long it takes. Princess has got to be inside, I'm sure of it. We just have to find her and get her out. Or rather, Mrs Ponsonby has to – though she doesn't know it yet!'

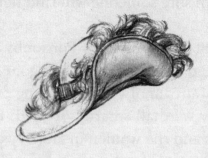

Eleven

'Just give us a little time. Please, Dad!' Mandy begged, after the taxi had dropped them off on the pavement outside Buckingham Palace. 'I'm sure Mrs Ponsonby will be coming out soon.'

'I'll meet you back here in half an hour,' Adam Hope replied, turning towards St James's Park. 'But no longer. We really can't expect Mum and the others to hang around in the park all day.

'If you three haven't found Mrs Ponsonby by then, you'll have to give up,' he added. 'Don't worry, if the puppy is still somewhere around the

Palace, I'm sure someone will find her sooner or later.'

'So what does this Mrs Ponsonby look like?' Casey asked when Mr Hope had gone, looking at the steady stream of visitors coming out of a side exit. They were all smartly dressed, the men in dark suits and the women in flowery dresses and hats.

'She's quite large, and she'll be wearing a hat with pink and purple ostrich feathers,' Mandy said. She'd heard Mrs Ponsonby describe her garden party outfit a hundred times. 'It should be fairly easy to spot her. And she'll have a little Pekinese dog with her too.'

A few minutes later, there was a shout from Casey. 'There's the hat!' she cried, as the pink and purple feathered creation bobbed towards them through the crowd. 'You can't miss it. There's no sign of a dog, though.'

'Mrs Ponsonby!' Mandy cried, rushing up to her with James and Casey close behind. 'Thank goodness we've found you. Please, we need your help!'

'Is there anything the matter?' James asked, for Mrs Ponsonby was looking decidedly cross. Her face was flushed and she was frowning as she marched along. Casey stared at her in amazement.

'I was not allowed to bring Pandora to the garden party,' Mrs Ponsonby said indignantly. 'I had to take her back to my hotel, and she was most upset about being left behind. By the time I returned to the Palace, I'd lost my place in the queue and all the chocolate cake had gone. And I only caught the merest glimpse of royalty!'

'Oh dear, that's a shame,' Mandy said, trying not to sound too impatient. 'But, please, we really need you to go back—'

'There was no earthly reason why Pandora could not have accompanied me,' Mrs Ponsonby went on. 'The party was held outside, after all. And on top of everything else, there was a puppy running around the Palace gardens! A puppy – just like the one you found in the park! Not wearing a collar, and quite out of control. Nobody could catch it.'

'Yes!' Mandy cried triumphantly. 'The puppy! That's why we need you to help us. Oh please, Mrs Ponsonby, could you go back and find the puppy for us? You see, we know who her owner is, and she's coming here any minute.'

'Then I shall give her a severe talking to!' Mrs Ponsonby retorted. 'It's quite ridiculous, letting these young dogs cavort about all over London. What can she be thinking of?'

'It's a long story,' Mandy said, 'but it really isn't her fault. She's Laura Dawson, a famous writer, and she's so worried about her puppy. Just imagine how you'd feel if Pandora or Toby got lost.'

'You're the only one of us who can get into the Palace gardens, Mrs Ponsonby,' James added. 'Please say you'll help! Laura Dawson will be so grateful.'

Mrs Ponsonby thought it over. 'I will help you,' she said eventually, 'for the sake of the puppy. And because I am aware that duty goes hand in hand with privilege. Luckily, I still have Pandora's lead in my bag. Wait for me here. I shall return!'

'Well!' said Casey, wide-eyed, as Mrs Ponsonby and her feathers sailed away. 'She is something else!'

'Has there been any news?' Laura Dawson said, rushing up to Mandy, James and Casey as they waited in a huddle on the pavement. 'Have you seen your friend? And what are you doing on your own? Where's your father?'

'Princess is in the Palace gardens!' Mandy told her excitedly. 'Mrs Ponsonby saw her there. She's gone back in to see whether she can get her out, but it's been about twenty minutes and there's no sign of her yet. Oh, and Dad's in the park with everyone else. They should all be coming back here any minute.'

'How wonderful!' Laura exclaimed. 'That means we're nearly there. George and Henry are safe at home, just round the corner. If only this Mrs Ponsonby can rescue Princess, they'll all be together again! I can't dare to hope . . .'

'She's a bit of a dragon,' Casey warned her. 'She might give you her views on puppies running around without collars.'

'Oh, I don't mind that,' Laura said with a sigh. 'It'll be worth it to have Princess back. And besides, in a way she's right. I know I should have had the puppies microchipped, in case something like this happened. I'm going to make an appointment with the vet straightaway.'

'Good idea,' said Mandy. 'It is worth it, and it won't hurt them at all.'

Casey broke into their conversation. 'There's Mum and Dad!' she said, pointing across the road. 'And your parents, too – and all the others. Looks like they've had enough of waiting for us.'

'Any luck?' Emily Hope said, as they all met on the pavement. 'We really should be making a move now, Mandy.'

'Oh, Mum, Dad! We're almost there!' Mandy said urgently. 'Mrs Ponsonby's seen Princess, and she's gone back inside the Palace gardens to find her. Please, we have to wait until she comes out again!'

Hurriedly, she introduced Laura Dawson to everyone before turning back to search for any sign of Mrs Ponsonby coming out of the side gate.

'We've heard all about the puppies,' Mandy's gran put in. 'But the thing is, we all have presents to buy before we go back to Welford tomorrow. Why don't we give Mrs Ponsonby a ring tonight to find out what happened?'

'I'm perfectly happy to stay here on my own,' Laura Dawson added. 'You've all done so much already.'

'Oh, please – can't we wait a little longer?' Mandy pleaded. 'This may be the only chance we have to see Princess.' She just couldn't bear the thought of leaving the Palace without knowing whether the last puppy had been found.

'I know!' James said. 'Why don't you go shopping here, in the Queen's Gallery next to the Royal Mews? Don't you remember, Mandy? We called in there on Monday.'

'Of course!' Mandy seized on the idea eagerly. 'They sell all kinds of things there – books, china and glass, and chocolates and biscuits with Buckingham Palace on. And model soldiers, too. Your great-grandson Tommy would like those, Mr Pickard.'

'That sounds perfect,' Adam Hope said. 'Nice and close by, and we can get all our shopping done in one fell swoop.'

So it was all agreed. Everyone who wanted to shop went off to the Queen's Gallery, and Mandy, James and Casey had another half-hour to wait with Laura for news of Princess.

'Oh, come on, Mrs Ponsonby,' Mandy muttered under her breath. 'Do your best!' What was happening behind those tall iron railings? Had Princess run off again? Had she been taken somewhere else?

Another fifteen minutes passed as they all waited anxiously, too tense to talk much. And then at last, Casey let out a cheer. 'I spy the hat!' she shouted. 'There she is!'

Behind the tall railings, the pink and purple feathers of Mrs Ponsonby's hat seemed to shine triumphantly as she advanced towards them. A Palace official opened the gate to let her through.

'Is Princess with her?' Mandy called urgently. 'Can anyone see?'

'Yes, she is!' Casey shouted, throwing her baseball cap in the air. 'Oh, good old Mrs Ponsonby! She's done it!'

'Princess!' Laura Dawson called, crouching down and throwing her arms wide open. 'Come on, girl!'

Mrs Ponsonby bent down to slip Pandora's lead from round Princess's neck. And then, in a streak of brown fur, the last little chocolate Labrador puppy came bounding across the pavement towards her owner.

'Oh, thank you, Mrs Ponsonby!' Mandy cried, taking her hand and pumping it up and down in her excitement. 'Thank you for finding Princess. How did you do it?'

'I applied my knowledge of dog psychology,' Mrs Ponsonby said modestly. 'And then I tempted her out with a ham sandwich.'

'I'm so grateful to you all,' Laura said, smiling as broadly as Princess. She buckled the puppy's collar and clipped on her lead before standing up, the puppy in her arms. 'If you won't accept any reward, then I insist on taking you all out, just as soon as Princess is safely back home. How about tea at the Ritz Hotel?'

'Tea at the Ritz!' Casey said, her eyes shining. 'This day is just getting better and better. Wait 'til I tell Mom and Dad!'

Mandy gave Princess a hug, and the little dog licked her hand. She looked thin and dirty, but otherwise, she seemed to be fine. 'So what have you been up to inside Buckingham Palace?' Mandy asked, taking the puppy's head in her hands and gazing into her beautiful brown eyes. Then she turned to Laura Dawson. 'You ought to write about Princess's adventures in your next book,' she said. 'They'd make a great story.'

Laura Dawson laughed. 'Come on, Mandy!' she replied. 'A pup at the Palace? Now who'd believe that?'

The Website!

www.animalark.co.uk

* Visit our great new website for more information about new and forthcoming Lucy Daniels book titles.

* Discover the world of Animal Ark!

* Find out about your prize-winning competitions!

* Try fun animal puzzles!

CHECK IT OUT NOW!

**Look out for Lucy Daniels'
exciting new series:**

Follow Jody McGrath on her travels as her dolphin dreams come true! Jody's whole family are sailing around the world on a dolphin research trip – and Jody is recording all their exciting adventures in her Dolphin Diaries . . .

The First title, *INTO THE BLUE*,
published in June 2000
– available from all good bookshops.